Brusilov made it easy for him by trying to escape in the cruiser.

Bolan's sniper's mind ticked off the necessary calculations in a heartbeat: range, velocity, the distance he would have to lead his target for a hit.

He took a breath, released half of it, held the rest. His index finger curled around the Remington's trigger, eased it back until he felt it break, then rode the recoil, eye glued to the reticle.

Downrange, a burst of scarlet splashed over the cruiser's dashboard. Without a seat belt to restrain him, Brusilov slumped to the right and out of Bolan's view.

Bolan didn't stick around to see what happened when the cops arrived. He had removed the viper's head, and while it would inevitably sprout a new one, that was not his concern this night.

The Executioner had another hand to play in the East Village, and he was already running late.

MACK BOLAN ®
The Executioner

THE EXECUTIONER®

DON PENDLETON'S

TERRORIST DISPATCH

A GOLD EAGLE BOOK FROM

WORLDWIDE®

TORONTO • NEW YORK • LONDON
AMSTERDAM • PARIS • SYDNEY • HAMBURG
STOCKHOLM • ATHENS • TOKYO • MILAN
MADRID • WARSAW • BUDAPEST • AUCKLAND

For Corporal Jason Lee Dunham, U.S.M.C.
April 22, 2004

First edition September 2016

ISBN-13: 978-0-373-64448-3

Special thanks and acknowledgment are given to
Mike Newton for his contribution to this work.

Terrorist Dispatch

Recycling programs
for this product may
not exist in your area.

Printed in U.S.A.

There is no place in a fanatic's head where reason can enter.

—Napoleon I, *Maxims*

I reason with fanatics in the only language they understand.
—Mack Bolan

THE
MACK BOLAN
LEGEND

Nothing less than a war could have fashioned the destiny of the man called Mack Bolan. Bolan earned the Executioner title in the jungle hell of Vietnam.

But this soldier also wore another name—Sergeant Mercy. He was so tagged because of the compassion he showed to wounded comrades-in-arms and Vietnamese civilians.

Mack Bolan's second tour of duty ended prematurely when he was given emergency leave to return home and bury his family, victims of the Mob. Then he declared a one-man war against the Mafia.

He confronted the Families head-on from coast to coast, and soon a hope of victory began to appear. But Bolan had broken society's every rule. That same society started gunning for this elusive warrior—to no avail.

So Bolan was offered amnesty to work within the system against terrorism. This time, as an employee of Uncle Sam, Bolan became Colonel John Phoenix. With a command center at Stony Man Farm in Virginia, he and his new allies—Able Team and Phoenix Force—waged relentless war on a new adversary: the KGB.

But when his one true love, April Rose, died at the hands of the Soviet terror machine, Bolan severed all ties with Establishment authority.

Now, after a lengthy lone-wolf struggle and much soul-searching, the Executioner has agreed to enter an "arm's-length" alliance with his government once more, reserving the right to pursue personal missions in his Everlasting War.

Prologue

Lincoln Memorial, National Mall, Washington, DC

The choice was obvious, when Oleg Banakh thought about it. Six million tourists viewed the shrine each year, according to the pamphlet he had studied while preparing for his final day on Earth. That averaged out to—what? Well over sixteen thousand visiting on any given day, year-round.

He had to kill only a fraction of that number to secure his place in history.

The homemade vest that Banakh wore beneath his thrift-shop raincoat made his neck and shoulders cramp, but it was fleeting, temporary pain. Each of its six hand-stitched pockets contained five pounds of C-4 plastic explosive, bristling with old rusty nails, screws, nuts and bolts added to serve as shrapnel. A nine-volt battery hung between his shoulder blades. Its wires snaked out to half a dozen detonators, twin leads trailing down his left sleeve to the simple detonator switch that dangled from Banakh's cuff. Add the Mini-Uzi slung over his right shoulder, also beneath the coat, with extra magazines filling his pants pockets, and Banakh was packing more than forty pounds of sudden death on this bright autumn afternoon.

The detonator, he had been assured, was considered fool-proof. It had two colored plastic buttons: green to arm the system, red to detonate the charges Banakh carried, blasting him to smithereens and Paradise, while any enemies within the killing radius received a one-way ticket to their special place in hell.

It was intended that he use the Mini-Uzi first, exhaust the magazines he carried if he had the chance, without allowing Secret Service agents or police to take him down before he had unleashed the C-4 storm. Gunshots would scatter any tourists who survived the first ferocious fusillade, but they would also draw in law-enforcement officers, ranging from street patrolmen to the special units that abounded in the nation's capital, protecting the fat, decadent servants of the Great Satan.

Folded inside the raincoat's deep interior breast pocket was the manifesto of his cause, three pages typed, meticulously spell-checked, all inserted in a plastic sleeve designed to keep the message safe amid the storm of battle.

Those who came to kill Banakh would be dealing with the other members of his team: five seasoned fighters armed with automatic weapons, each man prepared—make that *expecting*—to be killed before the sun went down.

A loyal member of the Ukrainian Autocephalous Orthodox Church, Banakh knelt before the huge statue of Lincoln, mouthed a silent prayer, then rose and set the manifesto carefully in place, well back between the giant's shoes, where it would not be damaged by the detonation of his vest or gunshots fired into the monument by officers outside. The message would survive, and if no one took heed, their foolishness would only bring more grief upon their heads, upon their families.

Banakh turned to face bright sunshine on the steps where Martin Luther King once stood and spoke of dreams unrealized. His hands trembled as he unfastened the buttons of his raincoat, drawing back the right flap so that he could grasp the Mini-Uzi on its shoulder sling. A woman standing nearby had watched Banakh curiously as he'd prayed. Now she clutched her male companion's arm and shouted, "He's got a gun!"

"I do," he told her. "And you haven't seen anything yet."

EMERGENCY RESPONSE TEAM lieutenant Rick Malone was wolfing down a meatball sub at a sandwich shop on 18th Street Northwest when his radio squawked to announce shots fired at the Lincoln Memorial.

Malone left his lunch on the table and ran to his cruiser, then gunned it from his parking space with the rooftop light bar already flashing, his siren winding up before he palmed the dashboard microphone and cut into the storm of chatter.

"ERT Malone responding to the shooting from the eleven hundred block of 18th Street Northwest. My ETA is ten minutes, with any luck."

"Copy that, Lieutenant," the dispatcher answered back. "Your team's en route."

Ten minutes if his luck held, and how many tourists would be killed or wounded in that span of time? Malone knew that depended largely on the shooter's choice of weapons, his—or her—proficiency with firearms, and the quantity of ammunition he—or she—was packing. In the country's present state, its fever pitch of anger, coupled with an obsessive love of lethal toys, Malone knew damn near anyone could snap at any time, for reasons only a psychiatrist could grasp.

Traffic was typically congested on the route Malone had chosen to the Mall, yielding reluctantly to lights and siren, slowing his progress toward the scene where people might be dying, even as he swerved around slow-moving trucks and buses, startled rubber-necking tourists, and sent cyclists clad in racing outfits veering toward the sidewalk. Three blocks out, with his window down, Malone could hear the loud *snap-crackle-pop* of automatic weapons fire. And not a single weapon, either, but a full-blown symphony of death.

OLEG BANAKH HAD watched two of his comrades die and wished them rapid transit into Heaven. The other three had found a measure of concealment—two in shrubbery around the monument's retaining wall, the third behind one of its massive Doric columns. Banakh was inside, crouched between the giant seated statue and one of the columns that divided the memorial's interior into three distinct chambers. Half a dozen bodies lay unmoving where they'd fallen when he'd gunned them down, and more were draped upon the marble steps outside.

Not bad for one day's work, but Banakh and his team were not finished yet.

He had already put the manifesto in its place. Now all he had to do was to wait for reinforcements to arrive, with television crews, before he took his last walk in the sun.

His mission was already a success for the most part. That was obvious from the wailing sirens, the flashing lights, the vehicles and personnel from half a dozen law-enforcement agencies gathered outside, below the memorial's staircase. More cars and vans, more uniforms and guns, were rolling in each moment. Banakh welcomed them, hoping a fair percentage of the officers would find their way inside the C-4's lethal zone.

So far, only a scattering of shots had been directed toward his hiding place, the shooters swiftly chastised by superiors. Banakh knew that his enemies revered their monuments to fallen leaders, drawing vicarious pleasure from the heroism that eluded them in daily life. Most would never join a righteous cause or fire a shot in anger, but it pleased them to recall that others of their species, long since dead and gone, had done great things.

This day, that changed.

Banakh glanced at his watch and saw that it was time for him to die. Smiling because his destiny had nearly run its course, he rose, clutching the detonator in his left hand, the freshly loaded Mini-Uzi in his right. His bullets might not reach the cars below, or any of the officers crouched behind them, but he hoped to keep their heads down, with some help from his surviving comrades.

All he needed was one final, shining moment on the stage, before he vaporized and vanished into history.

"Slukhay mene!" he shouted as he cleared the shadows, blushing with embarrassment before he caught himself and translated from Ukrainian. "Listen to me!"

Downrange below him, scores of faces watched from behind a hedge of weapons. Banakh started down the marble steps, ignoring calls for him to drop his weapon.

"Today," he bellowed, "you have an opportunity to learn from past mistakes!"

The first shot struck low, an inch or so above his groin. Banakh began to fall, grimacing as he pressed the detonator's bright red button and his world dissolved into a blast of white-hot light.

FIVE MINUTES LATER it was done. The three remaining shooters rushed the Secret Service line, spraying full-auto fire, and died without inflicting any casualties. Rick Malone moved up among them as the echoes faded, breathing the burned-powder smell of battle with an undertone of copper from the terrorists' blood spilled on the steps.

Or make that *sprayed*, where their apparent leader had been vaporized as he went down.

The blast had partially deafened Malone. Shouting orders to his ERT team, hearing them answer as they stormed the monument to clear it, he had time to worry whether that would be a permanent condition. That would mean restricted duty, if it didn't bump him off the job entirely, and he gladly would have kicked the bomber's lifeless ass if any part of it were left intact.

One of his agents stepped back into sunlight, calling down to him. The muffled voice announced, "Got something you should look at, Lieut."

"What's that?" Malone called back.

"Looks like the crazy bastards left a note."

1

Lincoln Memorial, One day later

What a difference a day made. Twenty-four hours after
what the media was calling "the worst massacre in the capital's history," Mack Bolan saw few traces of the carnage
that had taken place. There were a few chips in the marble
columns, which the reparation crew had yet to patch, but
otherwise the monument appeared pristine: no blood, no
scorch marks from a C-4 blast, no lingering stench of explosives or offal to send tourists scurrying off to the next
attraction. An untrained eye would never guess that nineteen people had been killed here, terrorists included, or
that fifteen more were suffering at hospitals around the
city, four of them unlikely to survive.

The monument had changed, however. There was no
denying that.

Throughout the day and night preceding his arrival,
Bolan saw that visitors had thronged the place, likely eclips-
ing any turnout for a single day since it was dedicated, back
in 1922. Many had come, he knew, to capture photographs
before the site was purged of bloody residue, although the
Secret Service and the United States Capitol Police would

have restrained the ghouls and kept them at a distance. Later, with the cleanup done, a pilgrimage had started, lasting through the night, not finished yet.

The signs were obvious. Along the rising steps, flanking a path left clear for any visitors who felt a need to go inside, mourners had left floral bouquets and wreaths in wild profusion, many bearing cards. Besides the flowers, other tokens had been left, as well: a dozen teddy bears in different hues and sizes, for the children who had fallen; Bibles, some of them left open to highlighted passages; sealed letters that would be removed, likely unread, expressing sorrow, rage and empty promises of retribution; several pairs of baby shoes; and standing tall amid the jumble, wholly out of place, a plastic pink flamingo.

Who could truly claim to understand the human heart?

It was approaching twelve o'clock, a normal workday, but there was still a crowd in front of the memorial. They stood in silence, for the most part, several of them gently swaying as if caught up in some private rapture, most just staring at the scene where people they would never know had died under the gun.

It struck Bolan that this was now a double monument of sorts. In the short run, before the public's brief attention span expired, it represented both a martyred President who sacrificed himself to save a fractured nation, and a group of strangers who, by accident, had stained a page of history with their life's blood. Their memory would fade, of course, as new atrocities demanded airing in prime time. The previous day's slaughter would be relegated to a thirty-second sound bite aired on anniversaries, for the next three years or so, until it lost all relevance to anyone except the wounded and immediate survivors of the dead.

"Bitchin'," a voice said, almost at his elbow. "Man, I wish we'd seen it."

Bolan half turned, taking in a pair of pimply teenage boys who should have been in school. They would have ditched to taste a bit of modern history, unmindful of its import. Raised on mindless action films and video games, they had no concept of mayhem beyond what they saw as entertainment value.

Bolan could have dropped them both without breaking a sweat. Two punches, lightning fast, and they would learn the stark reality of pain—albeit just a taste—but what would be the point? He couldn't save the wasted dregs of a lost generation, even if he'd been inclined to try.

And he had other work to do.

His visit to the killing ground was not coincidence. He hadn't been in town on other business—hadn't decided on a detour to sate his morbid curiosity. In fact, he'd crossed the continent to be there, flying through the night from San Francisco, but it wasn't any kind of gesture to the dead.

He was expected there, at noon, and had arrived ahead of time, as was his habit. That gave Bolan time to scan the crowd and traffic flowing on Lincoln Memorial Circle, checking for traps, looking for enemies. It was the way he lived, although in this case it was wasted effort. Only one man living knew he would be in the nation's capital this day, and that man was a trusted friend.

As for his enemies of old, the few who still survived, none even knew he was alive. Bolan had "died" some years ago, quite publicly—on live TV, in fact—and every trace of him had been expunged from law-enforcement files across the country, a concerted purge that left no file intact. If one of his remaining foes from yesteryear should pass him on the street this day, or sit beside him in a dingy bar somewhere, they wouldn't recognize his face or wonder, even for a heartbeat, if he still might be alive.

For all intents and purposes, he had ceased to exist.

Which didn't mean he was a ghost, by any means. He could reach out and touch his foes anytime he wanted to. Then *they* became the ghosts.

"It's something, eh?" a new voice, at his other elbow, said.

"Something," Bolan granted, with a sidelong glance at his friend Hal Brognola, who was a high-ranking honcho in the Justice Department.

"Let's take a walk," the big Fed said.

"I thought you'd never ask," Bolan replied.

They walked, clearing the crowd of pilgrims, moving east toward the Reflecting Pool that stretched for more than one-third of a mile through the heart of the National Mall, between the Lincoln Memorial and the towering Washington Monument. Brognola waited until they had some breathing room before he spoke again.

"You've followed all of this, I guess."

"I caught some of the live footage in Frisco," Bolan said, "and got the rest while I was in the air. They talked about Ukrainians on CNN."

"And they were right, for once."

"Some kind of manifesto left behind?"

"That leaked out of the Capital Police," Brognola groused. "When I find out who let it slip, there will be consequences."

Bolan let that go by, waiting for Brognola to fill him in. Another moment passed before his second-oldest living friend asked, "How much do you know about the war that they've got going in Ukraine?"

"Started in April 2014," Bolan answered, "spinning off their February revolution against what's-his-name, Yanukovych?"

"That's him."

"Russia weighed in to crush protests against the old regime, and that caused wider rifts within the government. By

March, pro-Russian mobs were clashing with antigovernment marchers all over the country, organizing paramilitary outfits on both sides. Russian regulars crossed the border in August, then they tried a cease-fire in September. Didn't get far with it. In November, separatists won a big election in the eastern sector, a place that sounds like 'Dumbass.'"

"Donbass," Brognola corrected, smiling.

"Right. Which brought pro-Russian forces out in strength, supposedly directed by more regulars the Russian president was slipping in illegally."

"Forget 'supposedly,'" Brognola said. "He's in it up to his eyebrows."

"So, today you've got militias, warlords, regulars, all at each other's throats, with normal folks caught in the middle. Russian troops are massed along the border, and Ukraine's responding in kind. Is that about the size of it?"

The big Fed nodded, then asked another question. "What about Crimea?"

"A peninsula south of Ukraine and east of Russia," Bolan said, feeling a bit as if he was back in his ninth grade geography class. "Disputed territory going back through history, for its strategic value. Seaports and natural gas fields. A majority of the population are ethnic Russians, but Ukrainians controlled the government until they got distracted by their February revolution. In March, something like 96 percent of voters backed a referendum to split with Ukraine and become part of Russia. The UN and the European Union ruled the referendum fraudulent. Russian regulars 'temporarily' occupied Crimea in April and haven't gone home yet. Pro-Ukrainian resistance groups are putting up a fight."

"Correct," Brognola said. "Which brings us back to yesterday. The pricks who pulled it off claimed affiliation with the Right Sector, a Ukrainian nationalist party founded in November 2013. Depending on who you ask, their political orientation ranges from ultra-conservative to neo-fascist. They call their paramilitary arm the Volunteered Ukrainian Corps. It acts in conjunction with terrorist groups such as White Hammer, accused of perpetrating war crimes."

"What's their angle in the States?" Bolan inquired.

"Long story short, they've been clamoring for military aid, getting nowhere with Congress or the White House—one rare thing that the White House and Republicans agree on. Their half-assed manifesto boils down to a blackmail note. More incidents like yesterday unless we arm their side and put them on a par with Russia's regulars."

"Which isn't happening," Bolan surmised.

"Not even close."

"They need discouraging."

"And then some," Brognola confirmed. "Our only lead, so far, is to an outfit in Manhattan's East Village led by a transplanted gangster named Stepan Melnyk."

"Never heard of him," Bolan said.

"I'm not surprised. He swings a big stick in Little Ukraine there, but he hasn't made much headway so far, butting heads with the *russkaya mafiya* operating out of Brighton Beach. Melnyk says he's apolitical, of course, but ATF's connected him to gunrunning between New Jersey and Kiev."

"Why don't they bust him?"

"It's all tenuous, as usual. The Coast Guard grabbed a shipment six or seven months ago, some hardware stolen from Fort Dix, but nothing in the paperwork could hang Melnyk. If his small fry take a fall, they keep their mouths shut. Or they die. Simple and tidy."

"And you think he armed the crew from yesterday?"

"Call it a hunch. We know he's in communication with his old homeboys. From there, it's just a short step to the Right Sector."

"I'll need more details," Bolan said.

"I've got you covered." Brognola removed a memory stick from an inside pocket of his coat and handed it to Bolan. "Everything we have is on there—Melnyk and the Russian opposition, Stepan's buddies in the old country. If you have any questions…"

"I know where to find you," Bolan said.

"Still doing business at the same old stand," Brognola said.

"I'll leave tonight, after I pick up some equipment."

"Going to load up at the Farm?" the big Fed inquired. In addition to his Justice Department duties, Brognola was the director of the clandestine Sensitive Operations Group, based at Stony Man Farm, Virginia.

"Nope. But I'll stock up in Virginia. It keeps things simple."

"Glory, hallelujah. So, you're driving up?"

"Three hours, give or take. I'll be in town by dinnertime."

"Bon appétit," Brognola said.

Arlington, Virginia

VIRGINIA WAS ADMIRED or hated for its gun laws, all depending on a person's point of view. No permit was required to purchase any firearm, or to carry one exposed within a public venue. Permits were required to carry hidden pistols—unless, of course, it was stashed in the glove compartment of a person's car, in which case it was permissible. Background checks on out-of-state buyers was a measly five dollars, conducted by computer at the time of sale without a pesky waiting period, which made the Old Dominion State a magnet for gangbangers throughout the Northeast.

Bolan had no problem at the gun shop he selected, located

in a strip mall on Washington Boulevard. He walked in with
cash and a New York driver's license in the name of Matthew Cooper, who had no arrests, convictions, or outstand-
ing warrants listed with Virginia's state police or the FBI's
National Crime Information Center. Twenty minutes later he
walked out with a Colt AR-15 carbine; a Remington Model
700 rifle chambered in .300 Magnum Winchester ammo,
mounted with a Leupold Mark 4 LR/T 3.5-10 x 40 mm scope;
a Remington Model 870 pump-action shotgun; a Glock 23
pistol chambered in .40 S&W ammo, plus a shoulder holster and enough spare rounds and magazines to start a war.

Which was exactly what he had in mind.

Before he started, though, he needed sustenance and information. For the food, he chose a drive-through burger
joint two blocks away from the gun store, bought three
cheeseburgers with everything, a chocolate shake and fries.
He chowed down in the parking lot, his laptop open on the
shotgun seat, and reviewed Brognola's files, which provided background information on the outfit he was tackling.

First up was Stepan Melnyk in Manhattan's East Village,
a neighborhood known as "Little Ukraine" for its latest in-
flux of expatriates. Melnyk was forty-five, had served time
in the old country for armed assault and smuggling contraband, then came to test his mettle in a brave new world.
Like most immigrant gangsters, he began by preying on his
fellow countrymen, running protection rackets, muscling
storeowners to carry smuggled cigarettes and liquor, anything that might have fallen off a truck on any given day.
From there, he had expanded into drugs and prostitution,
human trafficking, gunrunning—all the staples of an up-
and-coming hardman yearning to breathe free.

His number two was thirty-five-year-old Dmytro
Levytsky—"Dimo" to his friends—another ex-con from
Ukraine who blamed his arrests back home on political

persecution. The State Department had been mulling over his petition for asylum for the past four years, which Bolan took as evidence that they were either being paid to let him stay, or else were mentally incompetent—a possibility he couldn't automatically rule out, based on his personal experience with members of that sage department's staff.

Opposing Melnyk's effort to expand was one Alexey Brusilov, lately of Brighton Beach, a Russian enclave at the southern tip of Brooklyn, on the shore of Sheepshead Bay. Most people didn't know the bay was named for a breed of fish, not a decapitated ruminant. Mack Bolan had acquired that bit of information somewhere and it had risen to the forefront of his mind unbidden.

Brusilov was well established in his Brooklyn fiefdom, had defeated two indictments on assorted federal charges, and was well connected to the *Solntsevskaya Bratva* outfit based in Moscow, boasting some nine thousand members that the FBI could list by name. He was a stone-cold killer, though no one had ever proved it in a court of law, and had impressed New York's Five Families enough to forge a treaty of collaboration with them, rather than engaging in a messy, pointless turf war that would be good for nobody. The Russian's stock in trade was much the same as Stepan Melnyk's: drugs and guns, women and gambling, neighborhood extortion, smuggling anyone or anything that could be packed into a semi trailer for the long haul.

Brusilov's most able second in command was Georgy Vize, a young enforcer who was said to favor blades but didn't mind a good old-fashioned gunfight if the odds were on his side. He was a person of interest in three unsolved murders, but willing witnesses in Brighton Beach were an endangered species. Raised from birth to mistrust the police at home, they'd had no better luck with New York's finest on arrival in the Big Apple and mostly kept their stories to themselves.

Why stick your neck out, when the mobsters only killed each other, anyway?

And if they iced one of your neighbors by mistake, that was life.

Bolan saw opportunity in the uneasiness between Melnyk and Brusilov. It was the kind of rift that he could work with, maybe widen and exploit with careful handling, playing one side off against the other. War was bad for business in the underworld, but it was good for Bolan, just as long as he could keep the blood from slopping over onto innocents.

And that could be a problem, sure, since neither the Russians nor the Ukrainians were known for their discrimination when the bullets started to fly. Where an older generation of the Mob had certain basic rules, albeit often honored more in the breach than in the observance, Baltic gangs had more in common with outlaws from south of the border. They were full-bore savages, respecters of no one and nothing, as likely to wipe out a family as to bide their time and take down one offending member on his own.

So Bolan had his work cut out for him, and that was nothing new.

He finished off his last burger and hit the road.

Northbound on Interstate 95

THE MAIN DRAG from Washington, DC, to New York City was the I-95, a more or less straight shot for 225 miles, four hours' steady driving at the posted legal speed.

Bolan used the travel time to think and plan, which were not necessarily the same thing. Planning was a kind of thinking, sure, but it required at least some basic information on terrain, opposing personnel, police proximity and average response time. Even weather factored in. A wild-ass warrior pulling raids with nothing in his head but hope and good intentions might as well eliminate the middleman and simply shoot himself.

Bolan's rented Mazda CX-5 had a full tank when he started rolling north from Washington, meaning he wouldn't have to stop along the way. He wore the Glock and had his long guns on the floor behind the driver's seat, concealed inside a cheap golf bag he'd bought in Arlington, midway between the gun shop and the burger joint. The small crossover SUV had GPS and cruise control, two less things for him to think about while he was looking forward to the shitstorm in New York.

Brognola's digital files included various addresses and phone numbers, both for Melnyk's gang and Brusilov's, along with photos of the major players on both sides. Bolan could find their homes and hangouts when he needed to, plot them on Google Maps and make his final recon when he reached the target sites, to maximize results and minimize civilian risks. An app on Bolan's smartphone had the city's precinct houses plotted for easy reference and made him wonder, as he always did, how seventy-seven patrol districts wound up being numbered 1 through 123.

Go figure.

He had certain basic limitations, going in. Bolan's weapon selection in Virginia covered close assaults and sniping from a distance, but he'd had no access to explosives or Class III weapons: full-auto, suppressors and so on. He could absolutely work with what he had and make it count, but tools dictated tactics on the battlefield, as much as the terrain and numbers on the opposition's side.

The good news: Bolan had a built-in conflict he could work with, Russians and Ukrainians reflecting the eternal strife between their homelands. They had lit the fuse already. Bolan's challenge was to keep it sizzling, fan the flames and do his utmost to direct the final blast so that it damaged only those deserving retribution.

Making things more difficult, while waging war on two fronts, was the fact that Bolan also had to gather intel on Stepan Melnyk's connection to the massacre in Washington. If the man had supplied the tools, as Hal suspected, was it strictly business, a labor of love, or a mixture of both?

Behind that question lurked a larger one. The conflict in Ukraine had been confused from the beginning, talking heads on television squabbling over whether Russia planned the whole thing as a power play or simply took advantage of a split within its former subject country. On the ground inside Ukraine and in Crimea, both sides longed for US intervention to assist in the destruction of their enemies, but military aid had been withheld so far, as much because of gridlock in DC as obvious concern about the right or wrong of it.

Could the attack in Washington have been a false flag operation? Viewed from one perspective, it made sense: unleash a handful of Ukrainian fanatics in the US capital, to swing the people and the government against their side. Whether America weighed in against the rebels overseas with military force or simply closed its eyes to Russia's not-so-covert moves against them, the result would be identical, handing the independence movement yet another grim defeat.

That wasn't Bolan's problem, on the face of it. He couldn't solve the troubles in Ukraine that dated back to sixteen-hundred-something, any more than he could cure the common cold. Bolan was not a diplomat, much less a peacekeeper. He was a man of war—The Executioner—and he had a specific job to do, first in New York, then following the bloody bread crumbs eastward, settling accounts as he proceeded.

By the time Bolan got to Newark, he had a sequence of events in mind. It was a plan of sorts, but flexible, bearing in mind that things would start to shift and change the moment that he squeezed a trigger for the first time. Nothing would be static, much less guaranteed. The battle would unfold, and Bolan would be swept along with it, correcting course whenever he could manage to, otherwise going with the flow until it crested and the losers drowned in blood.

It was familiar territory. Names and faces changed, but otherwise it felt like coming home.

2

East Village, Manhattan

The hub of Ukrainian culture in New York City—known for decades as "Little Ukraine"—was located in the neighborhood of East Village. An estimated sixty thousand immigrants inhabited the area immediately after World War II, and while that population dispersed throughout Manhattan's five boroughs over time, two-thirds of the city's eighty thousand ethnic Ukrainians still remained in the old neighborhood, with its familiar markets, restaurants and shops, dwelling in the shadows cast by All Saints Ukrainian Orthodox Church and St. George's Ukrainian Catholic Church.

Like any other group of new arrivals, from the first European colonists to the latest Hispanic and Afro-Caribbean waves, the vast majority of Ukrainian immigrants were hardworking, law-abiding individuals with nothing on their minds except adapting to the land of opportunity. And just as certainly, a small minority were criminals at home, maintaining that tradition in the country they had adopted.

Mack Bolan had his sights fixed on that clique, as he

launched his campaign in Little Ukraine on a crisp autumn evening, around the dinner hour.

His target, chosen from the list Hal Brognola had provided, was a restaurant on East Sixth Street, halfway down toward Avenue B. The place was called The Hungry Wolf, known as a favored hangout for the thugs who served Stepan Melnyk. Bolan's drive-by recon had revealed that the restaurant was closed to walk-in diners for a private party. Two men on the door guaranteed that no tourists wandered in by accident.

Was it a celebration of the carnage in DC? Some kind of session called to lay out future strategy? Or did the outfit gather periodically to let off steam after a hard week of extortion in the neighborhood?

No matter. They were in for a surprise, regardless of the reason for their banquet.

Bolan perched atop a seven-story office building opposite The Hungry Wolf, with a clear view inside the restaurant through two large plate-glass windows. Peering through the Leupold sight mounted on his Remington bolt-action rifle, he felt almost like a guest invited to the party, moving in among the four- and six-man tables, touching-close but unseen by the men whose night he meant to spoil.

For some, it would be their last night on Earth.

The Model 700 was not designed with war in mind, though Remington did sell a special "Entry Package" model for urban police departments, and the US Army had adopted an altered version, dubbed the M24 Sniper Weapon System in military speak, for long-range use in combat. Bolan's civilian version held four .300 Winchester Magnum rounds, one in the chamber and three in a round-hinged floorplate magazine. Its barrel measured twenty-four inches and could send a 220-grain bullet downrange at a velocity of 2,850 feet per second, striking with 3,908 foot-pounds of cataclysmic energy.

All good news for a sniper on the go.

Bolan had been in place awhile, spotting the restaurant's arrivals as they entered, scanning faces already seated at tables when he took his post. Stepan Melnyk was nowhere to be seen, but Dmytro Levytsky was making the rounds, slapping shoulders and laughing at jokes from his soldiers, here and there bending to whisper in ears. A maître d' in a tuxedo loitered on the sidelines, muttering to waiters as they passed, dispersing drinks and appetizers. No one on the staff looked happy to be there, but they were working quietly, efficiently, focused entirely on the task at hand, avoiding eye contact with any of their customers.

Bolan did not plan a sustained attack, his first time out, but he had four spare cartridges lined up beside him on the rooftop for a quick reload if time allowed. The shooting would be loud, and there'd be no mistaking it for anything mundane, such as a vehicle's backfire in the street. Once he began, there'd be no stopping until Bolan disengaged and fled the scene, hopefully well ahead of any armed pursuit.

He scoped the two hardmen on the entrance first, decided not to kill them yet, and let the Leupold scope take him inside The Hungry Wolf. He felt like one himself, at times, when it was time to thin the herd of savages who preyed on so-called civilized society. He wasn't bloodthirsty and hadn't killed out of anger since the first strike that avenged his family, many years ago, but there was no denying that eliminating vicious predators lifted a weight from Bolan's soul, if only temporarily.

So many goons, so little time.

He chose a laughing face at random, framed it with the Leupold's reticle, inhaled and let half of the breath escape as he began the trigger squeeze.

AT FIRST, DIMO LEVYTSKY thought some stupid tweaker high on meth had lost his mind and tossed a rock or something through the broad front window of The Hungry Wolf. It took another second for his brain to wrap around the fact that Trofim Kulik's bald head had exploded, spraying blood and brains in all directions as he toppled forward, headless, into his eggplant mezhivo.

Even as the others at his table were recoiling, reaching for their sidearms, Levytsky saw a second bullet crack the window, this one bringing down a goodly portion of the clean plate glass. Round two drilled Marko Shestov's pudgy neck and almost took his head off, severing the arteries and loosing crimson jets that might have made Levytsky laugh in other circumstances, thinking of a whacked-out Rain Bird sprinkler.

But Levytsky wasn't laughing as he hit the carpet, reaching up to push over his table, which gave him at least some flimsy cover, while his free hand fumbled for the Colt .380 Mustang XSP pistol he carried tucked beneath his belt, around in back. It wasn't easy, going for a quick draw with his right arm underneath him, as he was scared to rise and make a target of himself.

The rifle's third shot—it could only be a sniper, the Ukrainian had concluded—made a wet sound slapping into flesh, as more voices raised in snarls and curses from the restaurant around him. He could hear somebody puking, hoped it was a waiter or the maître d' and not one of his soldiers publicly embarrassing himself.

Levytsky had no idea where the sniper was firing from, but since his lookouts on the street weren't firing back, he took for granted that it had to be someplace high up and out of pistol range. Or maybe his two spotters, skinny Sasha and fat Illia, had already split, fleeing to save themselves. It was a damned pain in the ass finding decent help these days.

Levytsky gave up on the Colt, useless for any kind of long-range work, and fished out his cell phone instead. Job one was to inform his boss of what was happening, in case the rifleman was part of something bigger, threatening the brotherhood. He hit speed dial and waited while a fourth shot took out half the second street-side window, drilling someone who began to howl in agony, as if a real-life hungry wolf was gnawing on his leg.

It rang once at the other end, then twice, three times, and someone picked up midway through the fourth ring, growling, "Yeah?" Levytsky knew he should have recognized the voice but couldn't place it with the world collapsing all around him.

"Put the boss on!" he commanded.

"Who is this?"

"Dimo, you dumb shit! Go get him! *Now!*"

"Okay."

Levytsky thought the shooting might have stopped—maybe the sniper figured out he ought to cut and run—but then a fifth shot came, just as a deep, familiar voice came on the line, asking him, "Dimo? What the hell?"

"They're killing us down here!" he said. "You hear this?"

Levytsky raised his cell phone aloft, above the capsized table, actually praying for a sixth shot now, so that Stepan Melnyk wouldn't mistake him for a drunken ass. The shot came, answering his silent prayer, but not as he had expected.

When the phone exploded in his hand, it sent a hard jolt all the way to the Ukrainian's shoulder, as if some big ape had struck his forearm with a baseball bat. He yelped and yanked his arm back, half expecting that his wrist would be a bloody stump, but all five fingers wiggled at him when he tried them. Nothing broken, no blood on his hand or sleeve.

It was a freaking miracle—or damned good shooting on the sniper's part.

Huddled on the floor behind his fragile barricade, Levytsky asked himself, who *was* this guy?

BOLAN LEFT HIS brass behind when he departed from the rooftop, one shell anchoring a slip of paper to prevent a breeze from snatching it away before somebody found the sniper's nest. That done, the Remington tucked more or less beneath the knee-length raincoat he wore, the Executioner cleared the rooftop access door and hurried down the service stairs to reach the back entrance to the ground floor.

Two minutes later, he was back inside the Mazda CX-5, left waiting for him in the alley behind the office block, and rolling out of there. Bolan turned away from Sixth Street without passing by The Hungry Wolf to judge the impact of his rifle fire. He'd killed five men and used one round to spook Levytsky when he'd raised a cell phone from behind his upturned table, either snapping photos on the fly or letting someone on the line hear Bolan's shots to make a point. The raised sleeve of the underboss's sky blue jacket had been unmistakable.

One target down, a stone tossed into Stepan Melnyk's pond, and Bolan knew the ripples would be spreading even now. His next mark, chosen at the same time he had picked The Hungry Wolf, was the Flame, a nightclub that advertised Ukrainian cuisine, a wide range of flavored vodkas and a waitstaff dressed in traditional peasant garb. The Flame's backroom casino was not advertised in any guidebook, telephone directory or tourist flyer, but the players tracked it down by word of mouth. It was, of course, illegal in Manhattan, but it stayed in operation somehow, almost certainly because police were greased to look the other way.

Bolan did a quick recon on the place and found its two

back doors: one for deliveries of various supplies, the other
for a hasty exit from the gaming room, in case a miracle occurred and law-enforcement agents came to raid the joint.
Both doors were locked from the inside, of course, but that
was no impediment.

For this job, Bolan switched out Remingtons, taking the
12-gauge with its 7-round magazine and an eighth round
in the chamber, three deer slugs to start with, and the other
five double-aught buck. It was a guaranteed door-buster and
man-stopper. He had the Glock for backup, in a shoulder
rig, and three spare magazines.

He wore a baseball cap and kept his head down for the
camera out back, as there was no point in giving anything
away this early in the game. Bolan took out the raid door's
hinges first, two one-ounce chunks of rifled lead shearing
through masonry and metal. By the time he blew the dead
bolt out, the door was ready to collapse, and all he had to
do was stand aside.

The shotgun blasts had sparked a panic in the Flame's
casino, setting off a stampede toward the main saloon and
dining room. That suited Bolan perfectly. He didn't want
civilians in the line of fire, if there were Melnyk soldiers
on the premises.

He crossed the threshold in a rush, through gun smoke,
following the shotgun's lead. A handful of the nightspot's
well-dressed gamblers were jammed together at the normal
exit, those who had preceded them causing a hubbub in the
main part of the club as they ran through, men babbling,
women squealing out of fright. Behind them, shepherding
the stragglers, stood two thugs with pistols in their hands.

Security.

The man on Bolan's left noticed him first and raised his
shiny automatic pistol, hoping he'd have time to aim. The
Remington was faster, perforating the goon with buckshot

from a range of forty feet. The guy was airborne in a mil-
lisecond, hurtling backward, slamming hard against a wall
and sliming it with blood as he went down.

His partner broke for cover, squeezing off a hasty shot
that wound up somewhere in the ceiling, diving for the rou-
lette table. Bolan dropped and met him with another charge
of buckshot as he landed on the carpet, firing through the
open space between the table's heavy, ornate legs.

Bad move.

Counting the seconds in his head, waiting for other
shooters to appear, Bolan spotted a satchel underneath
the dice table immediately to his right. He checked it—
empty—and began collecting wads of cash the panicked
players had abandoned in their flight. A second table added
to the haul. Not great. That made it something like eleven
grand, but it would help as stage-setting and added to Bolan's war chest.

He was all about sustainable campaigns.

No slip of paper was left behind this time. He didn't want
to overdo it, and he was swiftly running out of time. Out
front, somebody would be on the phone, likely to Stepan
Melnyk rather than the cops, and syndicate response time
might top that of the police.

A moment later he was out, jogging to reach his car
and get away from there, seeking the next stop on his list.

"SAY *WHAT*, AGAIN?"

Stepan Melnyk could not believe his ears. He had to hear
Dimo Levytsky say it one more time.

"The guy left a note, up on the roof he shot from, across
the street. Our blue friend let me see it."

"So? What does it say?" Melnyk demanded.

"It's printed in Russian, like on some kind of computer.
I could read it pretty well, though."

"Dimo."

"Yeah?"

"I asked you—"

"Right, Boss. It says, 'You are finished in New York.'"

"Say that again."

Levytsky repeated it, his voice gone wary, as if he feared Melnyk would blame him for the insulting note's content. No worries, though, on that account. Melnyk already knew exactly who to blame.

"Goddamned Alexey."

"I don't know, Boss."

"Eh? You don't know *what*?"

"Um, well, I know we're having trouble with him, but it seems odd, Brusilov leaving a note like that. I mean, it points right to him, like he's signing off on it. Now the cops've got it, and they're bound to pull him in."

"He won't mind that," Melnyk replied. "They question him each time a babushka falls down and skins her knee. He's used to it. I bet he even *likes* it. Big, tough man."

"But Boss—"

"This way, he rubs our nose in it, knowing the NYPD can't do squat. They won't find any CSI crap on the paper, bet your life on that. He skates on this for sure, unless we hold him to account for it."

"So, that's a war, then."

"Five of our guys dead? You're goddamn right it's war. We gotta—" Melnyk's other line distracted him, a little cricket chirping in his ear. "Hold on a sec. I got another call."

He didn't recognize the number on his cell phone's LED display. Melnyk answered, a curt "Who's this?"

"Me, Boss." It was Arkady Cisyk, from the Flame club.

"Where you calling from?"

"The phone in the pawn shop, down the street."

"The hell?"

"We got hit, Boss. Some guy comes in the back, drops Taras and Dimal, then grabs up some cash off the crap tables and splits."

Melnyk's mind focused on the money first. "How much did he get?"

"I don't know," Arkady said. "The place was pretty full. This time of night it could be ten, twelve, maybe fifteen grand."

"Son of a bitch!" Another thought struck Melnyk. "Did he leave a note?"

"A what?"

"A note. You know, a piece a paper. Writing on it? Like a freaking *note*?"

"No. Was he supposed to?"

Melnyk bit his tongue. Dealing with idiots was like Chinese water torture. "Are the cops there?" he inquired.

"Just rolling up. I better get back."

"Play it smart, eh?"

"Sure, Boss. I went out for smokes and didn't see anything. Don't worry. I have it covered, Boss."

Cisyk broke the link and Melnyk switched back to his other line. "Dimo?"

"Right here."

"Some prick just took down the Flame club."

"Holy shit! Another sniper?"

"This one walked in, smoked a couple of the boys and robbed the tables."

"Son of a bitch! That Brusilov. What are we going to do?"

"Chill out, right now," Melnyk replied. "And then start planning for a trip to Brighton Beach."

BOLAN'S HAUL WAS thirteen thousand dollars and some change. Not bad for six or seven minutes' work, plus something like two dollars' worth of shotgun shells. So far, he had reduced Stepan Melnyk's reserve of troops by seven men, subtracted from an estimate of fifty. Bolan thought it was a decent start, and he was far from finished for the evening.

The Melnyk outfit would be going hard soon, locking down while Stepan mounted an offensive of his own, but Bolan thought he still had time for one more decent strike, at least, before he shifted to the second phase of his New York campaign. He had already chosen from the list of targets Brognola had provided, picking a whorehouse Melnyk operated on East Ninth Street.

It was a short drive—everything in the East Village was close to everything else—and he parked a half block from the target, between a deli and a Mexican *taquería*.

The sky was drizzling when he stepped out of the Mazda, perfect cover for the raincoat he was wearing, which in turn concealed his Colt AR-15. The carbine was a semiautomatic version of the classic M16, identical in every way except for the omission of selective fire. The one he'd purchased was the "Sporter" model, with an adjustable stock and twenty-inch barrel, loaded with a STANAG magazine containing thirty 5.56 mm NATO rounds. It couldn't match the parent rifle's full-auto cyclic rate of eight hundred rounds per minute, but the Executioner didn't plan on tackling an army division.

He walked back to the brothel, suitably disguised as an apartment building, and rang the doorbell, waiting until a well-appointed woman of a certain age appeared to greet him with a practiced smile, asking the stranger on her doorstep, "May I help you?"

Brognola had furnished Bolan with the phrase that opened doors. "I'd like a bowl of borscht, please," he replied.

"Of course," the madam replied, beaming at him. "We have a full menu of delicacies. Please, come in, sir."

Bolan waited for the door to close behind him, then showed her the carbine. "No alarms," he told her. "Your life depends on it. Play straight with me and nobody gets hurt."

"I would be happy to cooperate, of course, but—"

When her eyes flicked to the left, he swung in that direction, just in time to meet a charging buffalo head-on. The carbine's barrel cracked a solid skull and the man dropped. Bolan stooped, relieved the heavy of a .45 and tucked it in a pocket of his raincoat.

"Anybody else?" he asked the lady of the house.

"Only the girls and customers," she said.

"Okay, then. Where's your fire alarm?"

Confused, then frightened, she led Bolan to the main salon, showed him the red pull station mounted on a wall between two reproductions of Van Gogh's *Flowering Orchards* and Picasso's *Guernica*.

"And where's the kitchen?"

"Through that archway," she directed.

"Okay. Get the place cleared out," Bolan ordered.

"But—"

He triggered three quick rounds into the floor. "No dawdling," he advised her. "You're about to have a fire."

He left her to it, found the kitchen on his own and yanked the range's gas line from the wall. It hissed and sputtered in his hand like an unhappy viper, until he laid it on the marble countertop, secured beneath a heavy skillet near the microwave. Next, Bolan shoved a small soup pot and two handfuls of silverware into the microwave, set it to cook for ten minutes and headed back for the salon.

An exodus was underway, including sleek women in lingerie and filmy robes, accompanied by men in sundry stages of undress whose forms and features weren't the

type to normally attract young beauties. Not, that was, unless they paid up front and very well for the attention they
received.

This night, the johns were not going to get their money's
worth.

Approximately half the crowd had cleared the brothel's
doorway when the microwave exploded, touching off the
broken gas line. Thunder rocked the place, a ball of flame
erupting from the kitchen entryway lighting up the door
frame, spreading quickly to the wallpaper and carpet. Newly
motivated stragglers sprinted for the street, trailed by their
host, with Bolan bringing up the rear.

The madam stopped to face him on the stoop. "What do
you think you're doing?" she inquired.

"Whatever Mr. Brusilov requires," he said, and winked
at her before he left her standing on the steps, backlit by
fire.

3

Brighton Beach, Brooklyn

The Brooklyn Bridge was free, but Bolan spent seven dollars and fifty cents of Stepan Melnyk's money to leave Manhattan through the Brooklyn–Battery Tunnel, instead. It was North America's longest continuous underwater vehicular tunnel, stretching for 9,117 feet under the East River at its mouth, emerging between Red Hook and Carroll Gardens. From there, he simply had to follow Interstate 478 to the Prospect Expressway, six lanes leading south to Brighton Beach.

The seaside neighborhood was wedged between Manhattan Beach and Coney Island. Russians began arriving in the 1940s from Ukraine's third-largest city, giving the district its nickname of "Little Odessa," changing over time to "Little Russia." Known as a hotbed for the Russian mafia, Brighton Beach was first colonized by *vor v zakone*— "thieves-in-law"—during the early 1970s, and remained the outfit's leading stronghold on the Eastern Seaboard.

Bolan had skirmished with *vor v zakone* before, several times, and he understood their mind-set. Anyone who kept them from a given goal was in for trouble, frequently extending to the target's family without regard to age or gender. Any "code" imagined by romantic types who wrote about the underworld without inhabiting its sewer had no application in the real world, where the Russian heavies settled scores with blood and suffering.

A language Bolan understood.

Rackets in Brighton Beach were more or less the same as in any other New York City neighborhood—or any city nationwide, for that matter. Immigrant gangsters started out preying on fellow countrymen with loan-sharking, extortion, peddling drugs and luring young women into prostitution. When good boys went bad, the Mob helped them along, received their stolen goods and armed them to the teeth against their enemies, collecting "taxes" all the while from each illicit deal. When they were strong and rich enough, the syndicate expanded into smuggling contraband from other states and other continents, the latter commonly including weapons, human beings and narcotics. All of that was found in Brighton Beach, the only question for a one-man army being, where to start?

If Bolan had to pick one racket that he hated more than any other, he would cast his vote for human trafficking, a modern form of slavery. Any of the others could be rationalized to some extent: people loved to gamble and get high, they craved cheap merchandise, were fine with buying sex and hoarded guns they didn't need because it was a grand American tradition. Human trafficking, meanwhile, involved abduction, rape and forced addiction, turning women and kids into hustlers with minimal shelf lives, spending their last years in abject sexual degradation.

Bolan had no feelings for the slavers, other than contempt.

They could expect no mercy from him in the end.

His first stop was an address on Brightwater Court. It

was just another house, from all appearances, but this one was a house of horrors for its captive occupants. At any given time, as many as two dozen victims smuggled in from Russia, Eastern Europe and the Near East might be held within its walls while being "broken in," a process that incorporated heroin and rape around the clock to weed out any stubborn vestige of humanity.

The *vor v zakone* considered it "schooling," preparation for a foul career that, while short-lived for most, was still immensely profitable for its overlords.

Unfortunately for them, the scum who worked for Alexey Brusilov had no idea that Bolan was about to pull the plug and cancel "classes" in their "school" for good.

And any members of the "staff" he found on site were going down the hard way.

East Village, Manhattan

"IT'S ASHES," DIMO LEVYTSKY SAID. "A total loss there."

Stepan Melnyk ground his teeth to keep from screaming out his rage. He felt his temples pounding and wondered if a sudden stroke might free him from his misery. He managed, finally, to speak.

"One man?"

"That's what Oksana says."

The whorehouse madam. "What else did she say?"

"Not much. One guy, like I already told you, with some kind of rifle. She says M16, but what do women know?"

"Was he Russian?"

"That's the funny thing."

"Funny? *Funny?* You see me laughing here?"

"Funny unusual, I meant to say."

"So, spit it out."

"He didn't have an accent, the way she tells it. Just a regular American, okay? But then she asked him something."

Melnyk waited, then snapped, "Am I supposed to guess?"

"Sorry. She asked him what did he think he was doing there. And he said back to her, 'Whatever Mr. Brusilov requires.'"

"That bastard! It *was* him!"

"Not him, but—"

"You know what I mean, idiot! He sent this guy. Maybe the same one who shot up the Flame and the restaurant."

"Maybe. I guess." Levytsky shrugged.

"Who does Alexey have hanging around who works like this?"

"No one I ever heard of," Levytsky answered. "He'd have sent more guys, I think, except to snipe The Hungry Wolf."

"Meaning he's brought somebody in. A specialist," Melnyk extrapolated from the meager evidence in hand.

"Could be."

Most times, Melnyk enjoyed a yes-man, but Levytsky was getting on his nerves. "That's it? 'Could be'? You want to put some thought into this?"

Another shrug. "It's obvious. We gotta hit him back. Hit hard."

Melnyk nodded. "If we were sure."

Now it was Levytsky's turn to look surprised. "Sure? Who's not sure? The guy leaves a note in Russian, telling us we're finished, then he tells Oksana that he works for Brusilov. What more do you need, Boss?"

"Something."

"Well…"

"It doesn't seem a little bit *too* obvious to you, Dimo?"

"That Brusilov, he's always been cocky."

Melnyk could hardly disagree with that. The Russian

was an overbearing bastard who liked to laugh when he insulted people to their face, so they'd feel stupid if they took offense. He *might* be dumb and arrogant enough to leave a note, or have one of his shooters dropping names, but—

"What if it was someone else?" Melnyk suggested.

"Someone else? Like who?" Levytsky inquired.

"I've got two thoughts on that, but I can't prove either one."

"Let's hear them anyhow," his underboss replied.

"One thought, it could be Georgy Vize."

"His number two? Without Alexey signing off on it?"

"If Vize was hoping we'd take out his boss and help him get a leg up, maybe."

"I don't know. What was your other thought?"

"Somebody from outside."

"Like where, outside? New Jersey?"

"How in hell do I know?" Melnyk growled. "*Outside.* Could be from anywhere, trying to start a war that hurts both sides. Create a vacuum, like they say, and let some new blood in."

"Armenians," Levytsky suggested, his dark eyes narrowing. "I hate those sons of bitches."

Truth be told, there was no end of candidates when Melnyk thought about it. He and Brusilov alike had stepped on many tender toes while staking out their fiefdoms in New York, including the Italians, Irish and some Russian predecessors whom Brusilov had removed, feeding the fish in Sheepshead Bay. Then there were other ethnic gangs chafing to rise and conquer territory, even if they wouldn't fit: besides Armenians and Chechens—who were just another breed of Russian, when you thought about it—there were Cubans, Salvadorans and Colombians, even Israelis waiting in the wings.

Levytsky wasn't convinced. "I still say we should hit him back, before he hurts us any worse."

"Do nothing until I give the word," Melnyk replied. "We clear on that?"

"Sure, Boss. Whatever you decide."

But was there something hinky in Levytsky's eyes, as if he might go off and try some action on his own.

I need to watch that one, Melnyk thought, wondering if his trouble might come from *inside*, rather than without.

Brightwater Court, Brighton Beach

THE BROWNSTONE WAS a way station along a trail of abject misery. Behind its drab facade, atrocities were the routine. Its soundproofed walls held secrets locked inside and kept the neighbors from complaining to police—who got their weekly cut, of course, but who had to make a show of taking action if the straight folk bitched too loudly, for too long. Beyond the old three-story house lay routes of suffering that spanned the continent, carrying slaves off to Manhattan and Atlantic City, to Chicago and Detroit, Miami and New Orleans, San Francisco and Los Angeles, even Toronto and Vancouver, with a thousand other destinations in between.

The victims, brought here from their hometowns, sold by parents, or the tourist spots where they'd been drugged and kidnapped, would be women under twenty-five or children, either sex. They would have been selected by appearance first, and then with some thought given to their families. If they were being sold, that raised no problem. Otherwise, the spotters would be on alert for runaways and party girls, for wannabe celebrities, for the abused and lonely ones who gave off victim vibes. The hunters would be smart enough to pass on trust fund brats and anybody else whose families were well connected, likely to make trouble if their little darlings disappeared.

His latest target wasn't like the brothel he had torched in the East Village. This place was a lockbox, a chamber of horrors, with no clientele but a handful of affluent freaks who dropped by, now and then, to unleash their demons in private. What happened inside stayed inside, or went into the bay.

No knocking, then. No small talk. Bolan climbed the concrete steps and pumped two 5.56 mm rounds into the front door's locking mechanism, then kicked through it to a murky foyer, where a sleepy-looking thug was scrambling upright from a metal folding chair. He made it halfway, then another round punched through his forehead and he sat back down without so much as a grunt.

Bolan swept on, taking no prisoners. His gunfire brought two more goons on the gallop, one armed with a pistol, while the other held a sawed-off shotgun. Bolan dropped them with a quick one-two and started kicking doors.

Some of the rooms were empty. Others had bleary occupants sprawled on filthy beds, drugged out, some of them manacled. He left them where they were, no time for individual rescues, and watched for other guns along the way. A fat guy waited for him when he reached the stairs, blasting a pistol round into the wall near Bolan's head before a clean shot from the Executioner punched into the gunner's chest and put him down.

The second floor was empty. The third floor's rooms were mostly empty, but those that were occupied offered glimpses of unimaginable suffering. Bolan found no more enforcers, no one standing by to take a heaping helping of his fury, so he made his way downstairs and outside, palming his smartphone as he cleared the house.

He had the number for NYPD's Sixtieth Precinct, the cop

shop serving Brighton Beach, programmed in. An operator picked up on the third ring, laughter in her voice until he said, "Shots fired, men down," and spit out the address, then cut the link.

Seacoast Terrace, Brighton Beach

"So our cousin from Kiev is having trouble, eh? I won't lie to you, Georgy. This news makes me glad."

Alexey Brusilov was seated at his desk, inside his private office on the second floor of Café Moskva, smiling broadly at his second in command. Georgy Vize, by contrast, did not seem to share his godfather's excitement at the news.

"I'm hearing other things," Vize said.

"What other things?"

"Our friend at Police Plaza says the restaurant shooter left them a note."

"What kind of note?" Brusilov asked.

"In Russian."

"Ah."

"And so he thought of us," Vize said.

"So what? Lots of people speak Russian."

"There's something else."

"Tell me," Brusilov ordered.

"Your name was mentioned at the bordello."

"By who?"

"The shooter."

Brusilov considered that and saw a pattern forming. "Someone's playing games with us."

"I think so."

"We need to find out who's responsible. We need to find out, like the cop shows say it, yesterday."

"I'm working on it, Boss."

"Work harder. Faster. If we have to fight—"

His desk phone rang, the private line that only half a dozen of his top soldiers were privileged to know. It was Jakob Yary calling, sounding out of breath. "Hey, Boss! Somebody hit the school on Brightwater!"

Alexey Brusilov saw red but kept his voice under control. "Tell me."

"Four of our guys are down."

"And?"

"Cops are all over the place, and paramedics are taking people out."

"That's it?" Brusilov asked.

"That's it."

"Stay close. Find out what happened if you can."

"Okay."

Yary logged off, and Brusilov relayed the news to Vize. His number two blinked at the news and muttered, "Jesus Christ!"

"Who's got the balls to pull that off? Who even knows about the school?" Brusilov demanded.

"Our guys, of course," Vize said. "The cops we pay off not to notice it."

"And Melnyk?"

"Well, he could know. Sure. Why not?"

"He thinks we hit him, so he could be hitting back."

"Could be."

"The school is going to be a hard story to spin," Brusilov stated.

"Cops have to tie us to it first."

A good point. They would never find his name on any paperwork associated with the property. A lawyer handled that and laid down buffer layers aplenty. Still, there could be implications in the media, made worse if Brusilov responded by denying them. That kind of stink was hard to shake.

More to the point, he wasn't sure who'd staged the hit, although he had a pretty good idea.

"That bastard Melnyk. Maybe he should have an accident."

Vize nodded, scowling as he said, "It couldn't hurt."

Ocean View Avenue, Brighton Beach

LOAN-SHARKING WAS a staple of most crime families in America. Even those who made their greatest profits from the drug trade generally lent money in the immigrant communities where they began and where their roots remained. So many workers, families and shopkeepers need extra money in the new economy that lending and the violence that followed when a borrower couldn't pay his debts on time persisted in every city. One such racket had destroyed Mack Bolan's family, and so the parasites were always on his mind.

Alexey Brusilov ran his blood-sucking operation from a place called Brighten Loans. Whether the spelling was intentional, a pun or just a clumsy error was anybody's guess. The sign hung on a pawnshop, squeezed between a candy store and lawyer's office, both closed for the night, though Brighten Loans was going strong. Its windows, screened by metal grates, displayed fur coats and china, saxophones and jewelry—in fact, a bit of everything.

Bolan breezed in as if he owned the joint. He had a name in mind, from Hal Brognola's dossier on Brusilov, and dropped it to a slouching clerk behind the register, saying, "I need to see Nikita."

"Who's Nikita?" the sloucher asked in a heavy Slavic accent.

"Never mind," Bolan said with a smile, already turning to retreat. "Tell him you wouldn't let me pay the twenty large I owe him. Maybe you can make it up."

"Hang on a second."

Straightening a little, but not much, the Russian disappeared behind a curtain and returned a moment later, following a fat man with a hairstyle that resembled Larry's, from *The Three Stooges.*

"How come I don't 'member loanin' you no twenty large?" Nikita asked.

"You're slipping?" Bolan offered.

"Nobody slips twenty thousand worth."

"You're right," the Executioner replied, showing the pair of them his Glock. "I haven't borrowed any money from you—yet."

The sloucher reached for something underneath his dangling shirttail, growling like a pit bull as he made the move. Bolan put one round through his forehead at a range of fifteen feet, dropping him, which had a surprise effect on fat Nikita's bladder.

"Jesus Christ! You...you...you..."

"Tell me when you think of something," Bolan said, cutting him off. "Meanwhile, let's see the safe."

"You're crazy, man. This place has got protection."

Bolan stepped behind the counter and around the corpse. "I see that."

"No, I mean the outfit. They'll be on you like killer bees."

"You want to call for backup, be my guest," Bolan replied. "After we see the safe."

The safe room was a big, old unit, maybe antique, with Krauss Construction painted on the door in ornate, fading gold script. "You see it now," Nikita said.

"I'd better see you open it," Bolan advised, "or you can join your employee."

Wheezing, fat Nikita stooped and spun the safe's dial back and forth a few times, cranked its handle down, then waddled backward, opening the heavy door. Inside were bundled stacks of currency, denominations ranging from fives up to C-notes, with a hundred in each bundle. Bolan pegged the total somewhere north of half a million.

"Bag it," he ordered. "Take the big bills first."

Nikita rummaged underneath his cluttered desk and found a gym bag, filling it with hundreds, fifties, twenties, running out of space before he reached the tens. "This is the only bag I got," he said.

"It's plenty. You have loan forms here?"

"Loan what?"

"Some kind of legal papers, for the tax man?"

"Shit. Are you kiddin' me?"

"I didn't think so. How about scratch paper?"

"I got some of that. You want to write your will?"

"A loan note."

"What the—"

"Do it!"

"Yeah, okay." Nikita lumbered to his desk, lowered himself into a groaning chair on wheels, dug up a notepad and a pen amid the pawn forms spread across the desktop. "What am I suppose to say?"

"Write, 'I, Nikita, on this date'—you fill it in— 'loaned'…what's your guess, around two hundred fifty grand? Just round it off… 'to Stepan Melnyk.'"

Nikita swore. "You ain't no Stepan Melnyk."

"Write it now and worry later."

Staring down the Glock's muzzle, Nikita nodded grudgingly. He finished quickly, muttering, "The boss will kill me. I have to set this straight. Starting now!" The Russian moved quickly for a big man, groping desperately for an object under a pizza box.

"Good luck with that," Bolan replied, and shot him in the face.

"O'LEARY, MAJOR CASE SQUAD."

"Hey, Irish. You recognize my voice?" Georgy Vize inquired.

He pictured the policeman glancing quickly around the squad room, trying to make sure no one could overhear their conversation. "Yeah," he said at last. "You're not supposed to call me here."

"I got a major case for you. It's going on right now."

"I kinda got my hands full with this other thing. Your buddies from Kiev?"

"Same case," Vize said. "But now, instead of getting hit, they're hitting us."

"Do tell."

"Two spots out here already, and I doubt they're finished yet."

"What makes you think it's Melnyk?"

"Because *he* thinks we're hitting *him*."

"Well, aren't you?"

"No. It's someone else."

"And I should swallow that because…?"

"How 'bout because we pay you more than you get from the city? If that isn't enough, I've got some juicy pictures here of you and two sweet little—"

"Stop it! Christ, just tell me what you want."

"More pressure on the damn Ukrainians. Keep 'em busy. Make 'em squeal, while we find out who started this and why."

"You plan to handle it yourself?" the cop inquired.

Vize heard the eagerness and answered, "Maybe."

"Only, if we've got new players on the scene, it's something I should know about. See whether I can nip it in the bud."

"And get yourself a nice promotion, eh?"

"Serve and protect," the detective said, almost chuckling.

Thinking quickly, Vize replied, "We'll think about it, when we find out who's behind it. If it's just a couple guys, they'll likely get a boat ride."

"Yeah, but if it's something bigger—"

"Chill, my friend. I won't forget you."

"Right. Okay."

"Get busy now," Vize said, and cut the link.

He never ceased to marvel at the avarice of human beings, driven to distraction by their pride, lust, greed, obsession with advancement. Everyone, himself included, had that innate weakness, but Georgy Vize had learned to cover his, screen it from prying eyes and go about his business like a dedicated soldier.

Which he was, in fact. Dedicated simultaneously to his godfather, his Family and to himself. Why should he separate the three, unless his own needs took priority?

But someday soon, he thought, when just the perfect opportunity arose…

4

St. Mark's Place, East Village, Manhattan

Detective Sean O'Leary had his orders. Not from the New York City Police Department, where he'd worked for nearly twelve years and drew a salary of eighty-four grand, plus benefits. This day, his marching orders came from Alexey Brusilov, the scumbag who contributed another sixty thousand to O'Leary's off-the-books retirement fund each year.

O'Leary hadn't started out dirty. As a patrolman in the Bronx, he had become accustomed to the little bonuses that came his way, most of it trickling down from precinct bagmen who paid captains and lieutenants first, then took care of the street cops in their turn. He knew the great department's history, a cycle of corruption and exposure, followed by "reform" and more corruption, dating back to its beginning in the 1840s. Every ten or fifteen years a "new broom" came along at City Hall, vowing to clean things up. When the dust settled, a few cops had been sacrificed for the cosmetic value, and everything went back to normal.

Now, creeping up on two hundred years since the rot set in, O'Leary found himself in a predicament with no way out. He was a cop, had done some good work in his time, but he was owned body and soul by criminals. That wasn't how he'd planned it, but he knew he wouldn't last ten minutes if he blew the whistle, and besides, how would he get along without the extra cash?

So he was out, rousting Ukrainians with warrants he had sworn to under oath, citing anonymous "informants of proven reliability," busting joints he'd known about forever, just like every beat cop in the precinct did. They looked the other way, most times, because Stepan Melnyk and his Mob fed the kitty too, from street corners to judge's chambers. Sadly, for the Ukrainians, they hadn't greased O'Leary lately. He was still a Russian tool, and with the warrants in his hand, the raiders he'd dragooned to help him couldn't very well protest.

Their current target was a numbers bank—what the Ukrainians called *chysel*, which he found oddly appropriate—seizing cash under the guise of civil forfeiture. It didn't matter if the charges stuck or not. Melnyk would never see the loot again unless he went to court and proved the cash was clean, a neat reversal of the famous innocent-until-proven-guilty rule modern Americans believed was still intact.

Morons.

The officers he had on loan from ESU, all soldiered up in black like something from a futuristic sci-fi flick, were dragging five of Melnyk's people to a paddy wagon. One of them, the honcho, had a big mouth on him, shouting that he'd paid protection for the month and what the frack was going on? He shut up after someone tripped him "accidentally" and slammed his face into the paddy wagon's open door. O'Leary heard a *crunch* and guessed there was a rhinoplasty session in the lowlife's near future.

Two stops down so far—the first had been an escort service boiler room, with burned-out hookers on the phones—

and he had half a dozen more to go before sunrise. After the first raid, they had picked up stragglers from the *Times* and *Post*, along with cameras from two TV networks, which suited Sean O'Leary fine. It never hurt for NYPD detectives to get their faces on television or in the papers, most particularly when they had a secret boss to satisfy. Georgy Vize would watch the news, and he would know O'Leary had obeyed his orders, earned whatever bonus might be coming to him.

All in a night's work.

But Jesus, it was getting old.

Shore Parkway, Brighton Beach

MACK BOLAN HAD his eye on Georgy Vize. He hadn't quite decided what to do with the Russian, take him out or play with him a little first, but he'd been watching Vize's home on Neptune Avenue when the man led six shooters to a Lincoln Town Car waiting on the street and they took off, bound for the Parkway and beyond, joining the same Prospect Expressway that had carried Bolan into Brighton Beach. Vize and his goons were headed back the other way, bound for Manhattan, but they skipped the Carey Tunnel with its toll and caught a freebie on the Brooklyn Bridge.

Bolan was with them all the way, intrigued now, smelling something in the air besides New York's pervasive stench of smog.

Why would the second in command of Brusilov's Family be heading into hostile territory in the middle of a night when guns were going off? Maybe he had a special kink to feed, a little something on the side, but Bolan doubted it. Whatever Vize craved in that way was available in Brighton Beach. His Family made sure of that, whether the guilty pleasure ran toward sex, toward chemicals, whatever.

So, a mystery.

He trailed the Lincoln easily across the bridge, into Manhattan, where the driver picked up St. James Place, northbound through Chinatown and Little Italy. Bolan was taken by surprise when Vize's driver turned right onto St. Mark's Place. It hit him then. Unless Georgy had surrendered to a yen for staring at the East River by moonlight, he was heading into East Village. Hostile territory, and particularly now, when blood was spilling on both sides.

What was he up to?

There was only one way to find out.

Bolan tracked the Lincoln to the northern edge of Tompkins Square, where Vize's ride came up against a wall of flashing lights and uniforms. Police were in the middle of a raid, and Bolan recognized the address as a target on Brognola's list, a bookie operation he'd passed over on his first sweep through the area, before he headed out to Brighton Beach. A SWAT team had three men in custody as Vize's limo pulled in to the curb downrange and sat there, with its engine idling, Vize and his companions taking in the show. Bolan, a half block farther west, used field glasses to bring the scene up close and personal.

Five minutes in, he saw a plainclothes officer stroll over to the Lincoln, bending and saying something to the passengers in back. One of them answered and the cop nodded, glanced at his watch, said something else, then moved away. The Lincoln moved on, and Bolan following instinctively, sensing that he was onto something now, although he didn't have a clue exactly what it might turn out to be.

Vize had his driver pull into an all-night diner, climbed out of the car alone and went inside. He took a table by the window, ordered coffee and some kind of pastry from a weary-looking waitress and sat waiting, munching slowly, sipping java, killing time.

Ten minutes passed before the cop from Tompkins Square arrived, solo, and parked four slots away from Vize's Town Car. Glancing at the goons the mobster had left outside, he entered, went directly to the Vize's table and sat down.

Bolan wished that he were a lip-reader, but it was not a talent he'd acquired over the long years of his war. Instead, he raised a Nikon D5200 camera and started snapping photos of the cop and Georgy Vize, catching the cop full-face when he peered out through the window into darkness, maybe checking to be sure he wasn't spotted in the middle of his late-night rendezvous.

Too late.

Before he pulled away and left them to it, Bolan also photographed the license plate on the unknown detective's unmarked Ford Fusion Hybrid, the latest thing in eco-friendly policing. He could use it, with the facials, to identify his man and maybe get a fix on what was happening.

But he would need a little help from friends.

Szold Place, East Village

STEPAN MELNYK WAS in a rage. It wasn't bad enough he had the Russians trying to put him in a box, now cops were coming out of nowhere—cops he'd paid good money to, for God's sake—taking down his operations left and right, without a warning or a by-your-leave. He didn't have the first freaking idea what they were doing, and it made him furious.

Pacing the living room of his penthouse apartment, Melnyk felt his soldiers watching him, feeling his nervous energy and hoping that when he exploded they would not be in the line of fire. Better to be out hunting enemies, tak-

ing their chances on the street, than to be caged up with
the boss when he went off into one of his screaming fits.

"Where's Dimo?" he demanded, asking no one in particular. When no one answered, Melnyk rounded on them,
shouting, "I said, where the hell is Dimo?"

One of the men, a relatively brave soldier, lifted a hand
as if he were a kid in school, asking to use the toilet, and
said, "Boss, you sent him out."

"I *know* I freaking sent him out! You think I'm *stupid*?
Why hasn't he come back yet?"

"I don't know, Boss."

"Why not?"

"Um, because you didn't tell us where you sent him."

"Somebody call him." They were all reaching for cell
phones when he changed his mind. "No, wait. I'll call him.
Find out what in hell is going on around here."

Dimo Levytsky's cell phone rang twice before he answered, asking, "What's up, Boss?"

"What's up? *What's up?* Are you freaking kidding me?"

"Hey, Boss, I just—"

"Where are you?" Melnyk asked, cutting him off.

"South of the park. You know that place."

He did, indeed. It was another of his brothels, with a
small casino in the basement, both lucrative operations.
"Okay. So?"

"So, the cops beat me here. They're grabbing everything
and everybody."

Cops. Another burning wave of red washed over Melnyk, briefly blinding him. He clutched his cell phone so
hard, he was surprised it didn't crumble into pieces.

"Bastards!" Melnyk hissed into the phone. "What do
we pay them for?"

"Most of these guys, I've never seen before," Levytsky

replied. "They aren't from the Ninth Precinct, Boss. I bet my life on that."

You just did, Melnyk thought, and asked, "So where are they from, then?"

"If I had to guess, I'd say downtown."

Headquarters. Melnyk had his eyes in there, of course, but so did every other outfit in the city that could raise the necessary scratch. And he supposed that would include Alexey Brusilov.

"That Russian bastard!" he snarled. "It must have been him all along."

"What, Boss?"

"Get back here, Dimo! Move your ass! We got some heavy work to do."

Stony Man Farm, Virginia

AARON KURTZMAN'S WHEELCHAIR hummed beneath him as he navigated the Computer Room, rolling toward the workstation where Akira Tokaido worked his magic, heavy rock pounding his brain through headphones that he wore throughout his long workday. Tokaido claimed the racket helped him work. This day it let Kurtzman cruise up behind him, unheard.

Kurtzman, head of the Farm's cyberteam, tapped Tokaido on the shoulder and asked, "How's it going?" after his young colleague lowered the headphones, music rising from beneath his chin.

"I got him," Tokaido replied. "Nothing to it, with the facial recognition software, plus the cruiser's license tag. I'm getting his financials and his background now."

"Give me the *Reader's Digest* version."

"Sure. Sean David O'Leary, thirty-two years old. He's a detective second-grade with NYPD's Major Case Squad, out of headquarters. It's funny. Did you know that Major Case is separate from Homicide? They only handle big-time thefts and kidnapping. I would've thought—"

"O'Leary," Kurtzman prodded, bringing him back on track.

"Right. He's been with the force—or should I say the force has been with him?—since 2004. He's got a twelve-year anniversary coming around in May. Had so-so grades in high school, tried some college, CUNY, but it wasn't working for him. Left before they had a chance to flunk him out and joined the army just in time for 9/11. Did two tours in Afghanistan and came out with a Purple Heart for shrapnel in his butt. Joined NYPD on the rebound, and he's done all right so far, considering."

"Considering?" Kurtzman knew it was best to prod Tokaido gingerly, unless he lost track of a narrative and had to be reeled in.

"His jacket's fairly normal for a street cop in New York. Two civilian complaints of excessive force during arrests, both deemed unfounded by the IAD. You know how that goes."

Kurtzman did. The Internal Affairs Division could hang a cop out to dry for some minor infraction, but he also knew from personal experience that much was also swept under the rug by members of what New York's finest called the Rat Squad. "Unfounded" brutality complaints could mean anything from a crackhead's lies to a top-level cover-up.

"Go on."

"The real kicker," Tokaido said, "is in this guy's financials. He earns in the mideighties, pretty much the median for NYC, but he's a sharp dresser, trades out his old car every couple years. No family to feed, of course. He's never been married. Has a two-bedroom apartment out in Woodside, Queens. But…"

"Give it to me," Kurtzman said.

"I have to wonder why he needs five safe deposit boxes, all at different banks around the boroughs. Minimal accounts at four of them, to get him in the door, but what's he stashing?"

"If he's cozy with the Russian Mob…"

"Exactly," Tokaido said. "Smells like cash to me."

"Okay. I'll pass it on."

"And I'll keep digging for a while. I haven't checked New Jersey yet, to find out if he's banking over there."

Kurtzman wheeled off and left him to it, headphones back in place, the music's backbeat guiding fingers in their dance across Tokaido's keyboard.

The report he had for Bolan wouldn't be astounding for a twelve-year NYPD officer. Kurtzman was well acquainted with the huge department's history, from beatings and chokeholds to Abner Louima, Amadou Diallo, and the so-called Mafia cops: a pair of detectives who doubled as triggermen for the Lucchese Family until an FBI informant's testimony sent them up for a hundred years plus.

Every major department in the country was the same, to some extent, and Bolan knew that very well. What he required on this job, maybe, was a bit of leverage. Whatever he might have in mind for Sean David O'Leary, Kurtzman hoped the information would be useful.

And he hoped that it would help to keep Bolan alive.

Seacoast Terrace, Brighton Beach

ALEXEY BRUSILOV WAS TIRED. He wished that he was tucked up in his bed, at home on Banner Avenue, and wondered whether that meant he was getting old.

Hell, no. He was as strong as ever, still loved staying up all night and partying or taking care of business, but this damned day in particular had worn him down. He didn't understand it, worst of all, and that was eating at him, causing him to question whether he was slipping.

Since he'd arrived in the United States, there had been tension between Russian operators and the East Village Ukrainians. Brusilov took that as a fact of life and ran with it, encroaching on their territory when he could, but never pushing it to the extent of open warfare. Stepan Melnyk was a man after his own heart, putting business first, getting his licks in when and where he could, without lighting a doomsday fuse.

So, what had suddenly gone wrong?

Brusilov thought about the hits on Melnyk's turf, knew that the orders hadn't come from him, and tried to figure out what that might mean. Most obviously, Melnyk could have stepped on someone else's toes and pissed them off. Maybe that someone else was smart enough to spin it, make the Ukrainians think Russians were behind the raids and get a nice war underway, ravaging both sides while the instigator sat it out, waiting to pick up any pieces that were left after the storm blew through.

Another thought: whoever pulled the raids might be a Russian, either from another outfit—Uri Pavlov's clique from Bay Ridge, maybe Ivan Budker's gang from Gravesend or, and this was what tormented Brusilov, someone within his own organization who thought he'd been too soft on the Ukrainians, hadn't moved in and squeezed them hard enough to benefit the Family.

And if there was an upstart traitor in the ranks, who might that be?

Brusilov didn't want to think of Georgy Vize that way. They had been through too much together, in the Motherland and in the States, but if he let his mind be ruled by sentiment he might wake up some morning with his throat cut, or a bullet hole between his eyes. Georgy was smart and capable, up to a point, and he was not averse to treachery. Soon after they'd arrived in Brighton Beach, he had helped Brusilov depose his predecessor, drove the boat that took old Maxim Stefanenko, whom they'd called the Butcher, for his last cruise onto Sheepshead Bay.

So Georgy was a possibility. Who else?

Brusilov had two *brigadiry*, roughly analogous to Mafia *caporegimes*, who were smart and ruthless enough to go off on their own if they thought he was slipping, and would likely take him down in the process to minimize blowback. In that case, Brusilov supposed they would dispose of Georgy Vize, as well.

That was something to think about, but could he talk about it with his number two?

Decisions.

One thing Brusilov was sure of: though he hadn't started any trouble with the Ukrainians this time, Melnyk was striking back at him, assuming that he had.

And that meant war.

James Madison Plaza, Manhattan

BOLAN GOT THE email dossier from Stony Man, acknowledged it and read it by the light of mercury-vapor lamps while he sat in the Mazda, parked within sight of One Police Plaza. The file gave off its own ephemeral aroma of corruption, even though it wouldn't be enough for most DAs to file criminal charges. The good news: since he wasn't any kind of cop or prosecutor, none of that meant anything.

Right now, he had Detective Second-Grade O'Leary by the balls.

He dialed the cell phone number Stony Man had found

for him, let it ring twice before his target said, "O'Leary, Major Case Squad."

"Check your email," Bolan said, then cut the link. Five seconds later, he had sent through two clear snapshots of O'Leary in the diner on East Tenth, with Georgy Vize. Ten seconds more and he called back. This time, O'Leary's answer was abrupt.

"What do you want?" It was said in a hushed voice, as if he wasn't alone inside the squad room.

"Face time," Bolan said.

"Right now?"

"ASAP," Bolan replied. "You and your Russian friends are running out of time."

O'Leary muttered something, probably a curse, then said, "All right. How's twenty minutes?"

"Good enough."

"The Hampton Inn on Pearl Street has a coffee shop. How will I know you?"

"I know you," Bolan replied, and broke it off.

BOLAN PARKED IN the Hampton Inn's lot, spotted O'Leary's unmarked pulling in and let the man enter the coffee shop before he followed. A waitress in her early twenties had O'Leary settled in a booth, just handing him a menu, making small talk, when the Executioner slid in across the table.

"Menu, sir?" she asked him.

"Coffee, black, should do it," Bolan said.

"Awrighty, then."

When she was gone, O'Leary tried to play the tough cop. "Let's get to it. I've got paperwork up the wazoo tonight."

"Pulling that overtime for Brusilov."

"I'm busting criminals, Mr.... What did you say your name was?"

Bolan kept it deadpan and replied, "I didn't say. It isn't relevant."

"Some stranger tries extorting me, I like to spell his name right on the booking sheet."

"No one's extorting you, Detective. That was just a preview of the file that's going to IA, along with five safety deposit boxes. They can run with it from there."

"No matter what?"

"You're leaving law enforcement," Bolan said. "The only point in question is the timing."

"So you say." O'Leary shifted on his bench seat, maybe easing access to his sidearm.

"You could try it," Bolan said. "But bear in mind that I'm responsible for everything that has your Russian pals worked up tonight. And Melnyk's people, too."

"Say I buy that. You ready for the heat killing a cop will bring down on your head?"

"Why not?" Bolan asked, bluffing with an empty hand. "Your file goes to IA if anything happens to me. I'm guessing that you've seen *The Godfather* a couple dozen times."

The dirty NYPD captain, played by Sterling Hayden, was shot by Michael Corleone, then smeared in media reports for his alliance with the drug trade.

After glaring at him for a long moment, O'Leary asked, "So what's your pitch?"

"It's simple," Bolan said. "I just want you to do your job. Impartially, that is, treating the Russians just like you've been handling Melnyk's crew tonight."

"Simple," O'Leary echoed in a mocking tone. "Just lay my life out on the line."

"You did that when you started working for the Mob," Bolan replied. "Call this making amends."

"Too late," O'Leary said.

"I'm not a priest," Bolan told him. "I don't handle that end of things."

"Just life and death, eh?"

"Now you're catching on."

"All right," O'Leary said at last. "What is it that I have to do, exactly?"

5

Banner Avenue, Brighton Beach

The news was bad and getting worse. Alexey Brusilov had finally gone home, retreating under guard to leave his office empty, just in case the trouble that had rocked his Family for the past few hours tracked him there. His house was on the small side, nothing ostentatious that would raise a red flag with the tax people, but it was fortified against assault, with several nice touches added when he had the old place renovated, prior to moving in. His bodyguards were unobtrusive, but they never strayed beyond an easy shout from their godfather.

Georgy Vize sat facing Brusilov, diminished slightly by the massive leather sofa he had chosen, while his master occupied a matching recliner. A low glass-topped coffee table sat between them, supporting half a dozen guns. Their muzzles all were aimed away from Brusilov, toward Vize, which did nothing to ease the underboss's nerves.

"Melnyk hit us again," Brusilov said. "A carload of his people took down two of our guys in a drive-by, outside Siberia."

The nightclub, Vize knew he meant, and not the distant

frozen wasteland used for generations as a Russian penal colony. The news put a crimp in Vize's gut, but he endeavored not to let it show.

"Who were they?" he asked.

"Sergei and Little Ruslan."

As opposed to Big Ruslan, whose last growth spurt had blown away when he was five foot five. His "little" counterpart was—had been—nearly six foot six, a strapping soldier with a weightlifter's physique.

"I'm sorry, Boss." Vize could think of nothing else to say.

"Sorry? Why are you sorry?" Brusilov inquired. "You didn't kill them, eh?"

Vize blinked twice at the unexpected question. "What? Of course not!"

"Then there's no need for sorry," his godfather said. "Don't be sad. Instead of mourning, take revenge."

"We've got teams out looking for Melnyk," Vize reminded him. "And—"

He was suddenly distracted by the trilling of his cell phone, from the inside pocket of his blazer. "Damn! I better take this. Could be something."

"Something good, I hope," Brusilov said.

"Hello?"

"It's me," the familiar voice stated. "You sitting down?"

"What?"

"Never mind. I got your guy. Well, one of them."

"What guy?" Vize felt as if his head were filled with cobwebs, interfering with coherent thought.

"The one's been shooting up your places over there," Sean O'Leary replied. "You still want him, right?"

"Yes!" Vize snapped out of his daze. "But how did you—"

"I'll tell you when I see you."

"See me?"

"When I hand him over," O'Leary said. "That was the plan, right?"

"Yes, yes. But we have to play it safe."

"Safe is my middle name. I picked a spot already. You can take delivery and run with it, while I go on my way."

"Where did you have in mind?"

"The Brighton playground, by the boardwalk. How's an hour sound?"

"We'll be there," Vize replied. "And you shall be rewarded."

"Music to my ears," O'Leary said, and cut the link.

"Well? Who was that?"

"Our contact at police headquarters," Vize said.

"Irish."

"Yes. He says he's caught the man behind our troubles." Thinking of the recent drive-by, Vize added, "One of them, at least."

"Ukraininan?"

"Um… I didn't ask."

"It doesn't interest you?"

Vize wished the couch would open up and swallow him, but he had no such luck. Instead of answering the question, he replied, "O'Leary's bringing him to us. We'll have a chance to question him."

"Bringing him where?" Brusilov asked, hunched forward now, his big hands resting on the coffee table, near a pair of shiny pistols.

"To that playground, at the west end of the boardwalk. In one hour."

Brusilov bounced to his feet and clapped his hands, smiling. "I'm coming with you," he announced.

"You think that's wise?"

"Wise? I wouldn't miss it for the whole wide world."

Riegelmann Boardwalk, Brighton Beach

BOLAN WAS SET UP on the rendezvous before O'Leary made his call to Vize, already covering the sweep of Brighton Playground through his Leupold scope. There were no children and no tourists anywhere around, although he'd watched a drug deal from his rooftop vantage point, across Brightwater Court.

Away to Bolan's left, or east, some sleepless types were still riding the Coney Island Cyclone roller coaster, a giant Ferris wheel, drifting in and out of restaurants, or dawdling at the mural for the fourteen-acre New York Aquarium. Those night owls were beyond his line of fire, though not beyond the range of Bolan's Remington. They'd be all right, as long as they obeyed their first survival instinct, fleeing gunfire, rather than approaching it.

Of course, some of them might be ringers. Brusilov had not survived this long without learning the ins and outs of treachery. As soon as he received O'Leary's message, it made sense for him to flood the area with soldiers, sending individuals and pairs, nothing too obvious.

How many did he still have left, from the beginning estimate of sixty-five to seventy?

Enough to do the job, for sure, if Bolan didn't watch his step *and* watch his back, the Executioner knew.

The upside, if O'Leary kept his word, was that the Russians shouldn't smell a trap. As canny as wild dogs like Brusilov and Vize might be, they owned O'Leary, had enough on him to send him up for life and then some, if they didn't kill him outright. They'd expect him to obey and follow orders without doing anything to trash the status quo.

Two questions now: Would O'Leary show up? And would he adhere to the plan he'd agreed to with Bolan? It was always possible the crooked cop would cut and run, with or without exposing Bolan's scheme. If he followed through, Bolan had promised that O'Leary would be covered—but they both knew that he would be front and center on the firing line, if anything went wrong.

The trick: O'Leary didn't know how Bolan planned to deal with Brusilov and company. The Executioner had kept it vague, letting O'Leary think a SWAT team might sweep in at the last second, rounding up the Russians, carrying O'Leary off to some small WITSEC hideaway where he would cool his heels until he'd testified against the Mob. From there, after he'd served some token time, a brand-new life.

Lying to the detective didn't trouble Bolan's conscience in the least. O'Leary had already built himself a life of lies long years before they met by chance, and anything that happened to him now counted as just deserts. But if the outcome were to be a sudden death, O'Leary wouldn't pay that price at Bolan's hand.

At the beginning of his one-man war, Bolan had drawn a line he'd never crossed, and never would, in spite of any danger to himself. He wouldn't kill a cop. No matter how corrupt or dangerous that cop might be, he or she had likely begun as a blue-suited comrade, what Bolan called a soldier of the same side. He might knock a cop out cold, or set a trap that sent him off to jail where he belonged, surrounded by sworn enemies.

Survival of the fittest, right?

A limousine and two black SUVs were rolling south along Brighton's Second Street, toward the playground. At the same time, Bolan saw O'Leary's unmarked Ford approaching from the west, as if on a collision course. With any luck, they'd park together, opposite where Bolan lay in wait to bring them down.

As patient as death, he settled in to wait.

"I OUGHTA HAVE my goddamned head examined, doing this," O'Leary told his silent backseat passenger. "I'll be lucky if I don't get wasted, much less make it out of town."

O'Leary's passenger, predictably, said nothing in reply. That was appropriate, since he possessed no mouth, no tongue, no brain. The backseat rider was a dummy borrowed from the NYPD's police academy in Queens. Recruits used it to practice carrying a wounded or unconscious man over diverse terrain and under fire, to save his life. Those who managed it were one step closer to a badge and street patrol.

Up ahead, O'Leary saw the Russian convoy turning onto Brightwater from Second Street, pulling away from him since they were meeting on a one-way street eastbound, and drifting to the curb. O'Leary passed them, tapped his brakes at last and parked his car half a block in front of Brusilov's point vehicle.

"Sit tight," O'Leary told the dummy, feeling foolish as he stepped out of the Ford. In fact, the man-thing couldn't get out, even if it wanted to. The Ford's back doors could only open from the outside, never from within. The backseat of his unmarked vehicle had no cage, but since the dummy couldn't spit or even move, that made no difference to O'Leary.

Georgy Vize was on the sidewalk now, two shooters flanking him, and who was that just climbing from the jet-black limo? Brusilov himself, in the substantial flesh. O'Leary paused and made a show of saying something to his man-shaped cargo, then put on a smile and went to meet the Russians.

"That's him?" Brusilov asked without preamble.

"In the flesh," O'Leary lied.

The Russian boss started forward, stepping out to go around O'Leary. "I'll see him now," he said.

"Hold on," O'Leary cautioned. "First, we've got some business to discuss."

Brusilov stopped and turned to face O'Leary. "Business? What's this business that can't wait?"

O'Leary swallowed hard and forged ahead. "My bonus first, for catching this guy and delivering him to you. Every kind of shit you can imagine's going to hit the fan if anyone finds out I gave him to you."

"You think I tell my secrets to the police if I don't own them?"

"Cash on the barrelhead," O'Leary said. "No pay, no play."

Scowling, Brusilov went through a pantomime of patting down his pockets, finally announcing, "I don't carry money. People always give me things."

I'll give you something, O'Leary thought, but said, "Somebody in your crew must have some. This one costs five grand, all by himself, considering the risk to me."

"*Have* you considered it?" Brusilov asked.

"Five grand," O'Leary repeated, "or no one meets the Muppet."

That one almost made him laugh aloud—damn he was funny—but he had his hands full then, as Brusilov's men searched their pockets, handing bills of various denominations to their boss. It looked and felt like five large, more or less, as Brusilov handed it over.

"So," the Russian said, "we see this killer now?"

O'Leary stuffed the cash into a trouser pocket and said, "Let's get it done."

BOLAN WATCHED AS O'Leary talked to Brusilov and Vize, their conversation lost to him, although the Russian boss's body language was replete with tension. A dozen shooters stood around and watched, some covering their godfather, the rest eyeballing traffic as it passed by. At last, O'Leary turned and led his Mob paymasters toward his cruiser, where the outline of a human form was visible in Bolan's scope, through the rear window.

This would be the tricky part for the detective. Bolan had not dictated his moves beyond requiring that O'Leary make a call to draw his Russian cronies out of hiding, placing them where they were clearly visible. The business with the dummy was O'Leary's scheme from start to finish, and the trick—for him, at least—would be surviving once he'd done the great reveal.

O'Leary reached the cruiser's back door on the curb side, bending at the waist to open it, using the same motion to brush his coat back on the right and bare the automatic pistol riding on his hip. The dome light came on when the door was opened. Brusilov advanced, leaning down to view his enemy, lips moving in what had to be some kind of taunting salutation.

Then he froze, seeing a lifeless dummy belted upright in the car's backseat, just as O'Leary drew his piece and pressed its muzzle tight against the Russian's head. Around them, Georgy Vize and the assembled soldiers reached for guns, but even from a distance, Bolan could hear Brusilov commanding them to stop.

It was a standoff for the moment, but O'Leary had to know it wouldn't last. To drive away, he had to walk around the cruiser, dragging Brusilov along with him, past Vize and all those fuming goons, then climb into the driver's seat, fire up the engine and escape somehow before the Russian firing squad sprayed him with lead.

Damn near impossible—but it was not Mack Bolan's problem.

He locked crosshairs on Georgy Vize's head and sent 220 grains of death sizzling downrange at half a mile per second, his target detonating like a melon with a cherry bomb inside. Before the echo of his gunshot reached the Russians, he had cranked the Model 700's bolt, chambered another round and picked another target from the thirteen Russians still alive, one of the shooters who had pulled an MP-5K submachine gun from beneath his coat and held it ready, lacking only targets in the night.

Bolan's next round drilled through the shooter's chin, shattered his mandible and plowed into his spine, flipping his shaved head backward at an angle it could never reach in life. Blood sprayed in all directions from the dead man's ravaged face and throat, dousing the nearest of his comrades and delaying their reactions to the second rifle shot.

The goons knew they were under fire now, but still weren't sure from where, or by how many guns. Four of them stuck with Brusilov, guns pointed at O'Leary, each one looking for an opening to take him down. The others scattered, seeking cover from the cars they had arrived in, since there was no other to be found.

BRUSILOV COULD NOT believe the way his plan had gone to shit in nothing flat. He'd been too anxious, too damned hopeful. He could see that now, but what in hell was he supposed to do about it, with a gun pressed to his head and some wildman out in the darkness somewhere, taking down his boys?

He started out by talking to the cop. "You made a freaking horrible mistake tonight, my friend. You know that, right? Taking our money all this time, and now you pull this shit? You haven't even got a warrant to arrest me, or you wouldn't pull this sneaky crap."

"Shut up!" O'Leary snarled at him, trying to minimize his sight profile by slouching behind the cruiser, dragging Brusilov along with him. "I didn't have a choice!"

"You got one now, though," Brusilov replied, ducking instinctively as yet another rifle shot rang out. "Just let me go and drive away. My boys'll deal with the shooter."

"And you'll just let me go, huh? Just forget about all this?"

That wouldn't be believable, so Brusilov replied, "A smart man, in your place, would run as fast and far as he could go. That's all I'm saying."

"Shit!" O'Leary shoved him then, and turned to sprint around the front end of his cruiser, toward the driver's side. Brusilov snatched a pistol from his nearest soldier, saw it was a Glock—no safety to delay him—and began to fire before O'Leary reached the front left fender.

His first round burned through O'Leary's biceps, maybe penetrating to his rib cage, but Brusilov couldn't tell, so he kept on firing: four, five shots before his man went down, invisible where he had dropped behind the cop car.

Just then, death whispered in Brusilov's right ear, passing him by to strike the shooter he'd disarmed a moment earlier. Luka was lifted off his feet by the impact and slammed onto concrete, blood geysering out of his chest as his eyes locked on nothing and froze there.

Brusilov dropped to all fours, skinning palms and knees against the rough sidewalk. He peered around, saw half his shooters, give or take, hiding behind the other cars, as he was. He couldn't blame them for attempting to survive, but now he had to think about escape.

With this kind of gunfire, cops would soon be swarming to the scene. The Sixtieth Precinct was roughly a quarter mile west of the boardwalk, say five minutes tops before the first squad cars arrived, maybe another five before the SWAT team showed. If Brusilov was still there when the police showed up, he'd be tied up for hours, maybe days.

And if they linked the pistol he was holding to O'Leary's

death, he might be locked away forever, doing hard time in
some supermax hellhole for taking out a cop.

Brusilov shouted at his men, the ones that he could see,
commanding them to get up on their feet and fight like
men, to get in their cars and help him get the hell away
from there. A couple of them, younger ones, began to rise,
then saw the others holding still and sank back down, each
soldier clinging to his gun as if it were a holy talisman.

Brusilov cursed at them. "The cops'll be here any minute! We've got no time left to dick around!"

"Hey, Boss," a hulking thug named Mischa answered
back, "you know we got a sniper out there, right?"

"I don't care if we got a hundred of them. If we're still
here when the law shows up, we all go down for one dead
cop. That's mandatory life, unless they stick a needle in
your arm."

Mischa considered that, was rising to a kind of Quasi-
modo crouch, and died there as a bullet struck his forehead,
split his head wide-open. When he went down, Brusilov
saw his other soldiers cowering, avoiding eye contact with
their godfather, maybe praying this would all just go away.

Brusilov had a sudden thought. What if O'Leary had
been careless, left his cruiser's key in the ignition since he
didn't plan to linger? Just a quick peek ought to settle it. He
crawled up to the Ford's passenger door and chanced a look.

The key was there!

Grinning fiercely, Brusilov climbed in, dragging himself
across the shotgun seat, wedging himself behind the steer-
ing wheel. It was a tight fit, but he made it, firing up the engine and releasing the parking brake. Cackling in triumph,
he put the car in Drive and squealed off from the curb.

BOLAN HEARD SIRENS WAILING, and knew that in another minute, maybe two, he'd see the flashing lights atop squad cars
as they responded to the shooting call. Somebody on the

boardwalk might have phoned it in, or residents in some nearby apartment building.

It made no difference. His work was nearly done.

Brusilov made it easy for him, trying to escape alone in Sean O'Leary's cruiser. If the Russian's men had rallied to him, piled into one of their hulking SUVs, it would have been more difficult, more time consuming, trying to take out the man in charge.

But the Ford Fusion Hybrid was another story altogether. It was smaller, and its windows weren't blacked out like those on Brusilov's crew's wagons. Better yet, the rear right door was still ajar, which kept the cruiser's dome light burning bright, granting a clear shot at the man behind the wheel. The problem of a moving target complicated things, but Bolan's long experience behind a scope took care of that.

His sniper's mind ticked off the necessary calculations in a heartbeat: range, velocity, the distance he would have to lead his target for a hit. The driver's window, Bolan saw, was open, so there would be no deflection from its glass.

Bolan struck his pose and held it, welded into place by muscle memory. He took a breath, released half of it, held the rest. His index finger curled around the Model 700's trigger, eased it back until he felt it break, then Bolan rode the rifle's recoil, eye glued to the Leupold's reticle.

Downrange, a burst of scarlet splashed over Sean O'Leary's dashboard and the inside of his cruiser's windshield. Nearly headless at the wheel, without a seat belt to restrain him, Alexey Brusilov slumped to his right and out of Bolan's view. The cruiser followed his direction, swerving toward the park, jumping the curb and jolting to a halt when it collided with a lamppost.

Bolan didn't stick around to see what happened when the cops arrived, whether they found the other Russians waiting for them, or the living managed to escape. He had removed the viper's head, and while it would inevitably sprout a new one, that was not Bolan's concern this night.

He had another hand to play in East Village, and he was already running late.

6

Szold Place, East Village

Stepan Melnyk did not trust his penthouse anymore, despite the private access elevator that required a special key card for the swift ride up to the eleventh floor. He was afraid to step out on his rooftop terrace, with a sniper lurking somewhere in the night, and even with the drapes drawn over windows advertised as bulletproof, he did not feel secure.

It was a simple fact of life that anybody could be killed, if an assassin was determined and had low regard for personal survival. "Bulletproof" meant nothing in an era when fanatics stockpiled RPGs and Stingers that could blast through masonry as if the walls were made of tissue paper. Tight security on elevators mattered little when the law required that every building also have fire stairs accessible to any tenant.

For the first time since arriving in America, head filled with dreams, a suitcase filled with cash, Melnyk felt absolutely, dangerously vulnerable.

He had guards watching the fire stairs, naturally, three men armed with submachine guns who had proved themselves in battle time and time again. Two-thirds of Mel-

nyk's soldiers had done time in uniform back home, with
the Ukrainian Ground Forces or Airmobile teams, a few
handling dirty work for the Security Service. The remain-
der had learned their survival skills on mean streets in
Kiev, Odessa and Sevastopol, where life was cheap and
death came in a wide variety of forms.

Melnyk did not believe his men would let him down *in-
tentionally*. He dismissed the thought that any would desert
him when the fighting started, but he questioned whether
they were equal to the enemies who might be ranged against
them. If—

Dimo Levytsky barged into the room without knocking, a dazed expression on his face. Before Melnyk could
chastise him, he blurted out, "They're dead, Boss! Someone took them out. It's all over the news."

"Slow down, damn it. *Who's* dead?"

"The top dogs," Levytsky answered, beaming at him.
"Brusilov and Vize! More of their soldiers, too."

"When did this happen?"

"Just now. Well, I guess it must have been like half an
hour ago."

"Where?"

"Down by the Brighton Beach boardwalk. WGN says
they got a dead cop down there, too. No name on that one
yet, but they've confirmed the Russians."

Melnyk's mind was reeling. If his men had taken out the
Russian scum, he would have heard about it first, before
the news was splashed all over TV. And since his people
hadn't done it, who had? He'd been worried from the start
about an unknown player egging on both sides to fight,
but had dismissed it as the bodies started piling up. No
law-enforcement agency he'd ever heard of would attempt
something like that, and none of the remaining Eastern

European gangs scattered around New York were big or smart enough to pull it off.

Another question: Now that Brusilov was dead, was Melnyk safe?

God knew he didn't feel that way.

"Okay," he told Levytsky. "Before we start to celebrate, we need to find out what went down. The cops are going to come around with questions anytime now, soon as they put two and two together, asking where we've been all night and did we have it in for Brusilov, whatever. When they get here, we can't have machine guns all over the place, or any other shit like that. We all have to look normal."

Which, he knew, meant letting down their guard.

"I've got a call in to our guy at the Ninth Precinct. He'll contact me if anybody starts to make a move our way."

"What if the word comes out of headquarters?"

"He's got it covered," Levytsky said. "Two kids in colleges he can't afford, so this guy can't afford to kill the golden goose, you know?"

"It was the goose that laid the golden eggs," Melnyk corrected him.

"Huh?"

"Never mind. We need to—"

Sharp, staccato gunfire interrupted Melnyk, blew his thoughts away. He stood rooted in deep-shag carpeting and swiveled toward the source of that unwelcome sound.

The damned fire stairs.

WHILE EN ROUTE to his next hit, Bolan had stopped at an all-night convenience store to buy a two-liter bottle of soda and a roll of duct tape. He had dumped the soda in the parking lot, then taped the empty bottle to the muzzle of his Colt AR-15, creating a makeshift and barely adequate suppressor that should serve for one shot, maybe two if he was lucky. After that, it wouldn't matter, since the home team would be throwing everything they had at Bolan in their bid to take him down. Suppressors were superfluous from that point on, once hell broke loose.

Bolan was going in heavy. The Colt would be his lead weapon, the Remington backup, slung across his back. He'd have the Glock to settle any close-up arguments. The pockets of his raincoat drooped with the weight of extra magazines and shotgun shells for his three weapons. Getting inside Melnyk's apartment building was no big deal. There was a sleepy doorman on the street in front, but no one covering the rear. The elevator up to Melnyk's penthouse was secure, so Bolan took the stairs, assuming they'd be guarded somewhere near the top. That's where the soda bottle came in, and he hoped that it would serve him well.

He didn't rush the climb, pausing below each landing on the way to watch and listen for lookouts. Eleven floors, twenty-two zigzag flights, and Bolan guessed that any sentries would be posted at the top, or in a pinch on ten. Melnyk would not want neighbors blundering into his goons and getting spooked, calling the management or the police to register complaints.

And speaking of the cops, he knew they would be on their way to Melnyk's place, sooner or later. It was only natural, when one godfather bit the bullet, for detectives to interrogate his rivals. Whether they'd show up tonight or sometime in the week ahead was anybody's guess, but Bolan wanted to be done with this part of his job and gone before they came sniffing around.

Coming up on the tenth floor, Bolan heard the sounds of muffled conversation from above. He paused, made sure the Colt was ready and proceeded, one step at a time. As soon as he saw feet and legs, he slowed, then mounted two more risers, until he was looking at the first soldier's belt buckle.

Close enough.

He aimed and fired one nearly silent shot, gutting his faceless enemy, then rushed the others, and to hell with stealth. Speed mattered now, and making each shot count.

Bolan caught the second sentry with a 5.56 mm mangler to the chest, slamming him back against a concrete wall and smearing it with bright blood from the exit wound. Dying before he fell, the shooter still squeezed off a wild burst from his MP-5, sending a storm of deadly ricochets past Bolan, crackling down the stairwell.

The Executioner saw the SMG kick loose from dying fingers, so he concentrated on the third and final sentry on the staircase. The gunner was retreating toward a metal fire door, brandishing a Mini-Uzi, but he hadn't fired it yet, maybe afraid of wounding his companions. As they fell, he lost that last restraint and brought his weapon into line with Bolan's face.

Too late.

The AR-15 cracked out two more shots, the furthest thing from silent now, and dropped Bolan's last target where he stood. The guy fell like a sack of dirty laundry, and his Mini-Uzi clattered down the stairs past Bolan, bouncing as it went. Instead of grabbing for it, Bolan let it go, already focused on the door three men had sacrificed themselves to guard.

DIMO LEVYTSKY WAS on his walkie-talkie, shouting for the staircase sentries, none of whom were answering. He cursed them seven ways from Sunday, but it did no good. The gunfire had not lasted long, but the gangster liked the silence even less.

It told him something had to be desperately wrong.

Not cops. He knew that much instinctively. American police came in with warrants. They would have roused the building's super, commandeered the elevator and arrived in style, though almost certainly with people on the stairs, as well.

Hitting the stairs alone meant something else, and Levytsky knew it had to be bad news.

He'd left Melnyk with most of his gunners around him, all armed with Kalashnikov civilian models, modified to fire full-auto by an outlaw gunsmith in the Bronx. They would not hesitate to kill—or die—for their godfather when the enemy revealed himself.

One enemy? Or was an army coming up the fire stairs, drawing closer by the second?

Levytsky led his most trusted soldiers to the fire door, kept unlocked to satisfy the city fire marshals who dropped by unexpectedly, writing citations if they noted violations of their rules. He knew the staircase sentries should have checked in via radio by now, if they had beaten back intruders from below. Their silence told him they were either dead, or else so badly wounded that they could not warn their comrades on the penthouse level.

Call it three men down.

When they had nearly reached the fire door, Levytsky stopped and sent three men ahead. "Find out what's happening," he ordered. "Use your freaking radios, no matter what."

The point men reached the door, which had no window to permit a view of the descending stairs. It opened blind onto the landing, with a sign that warned escaping residents to check the door for heat before they opened it, perhaps admitting flames.

Melnyk's second in command stood watching, gripping an MP-5K machine pistol, while his point men opened the door and pushed it back, fluorescent light spilling across the threshold from the stairwell. For a second, Levytsky thought the landing might be clear, but then he heard the *crack* of a rifle, followed by two more, and his point men were taken out of play, dropping hard to the floor before they could return fire.

Two gunners edged forward, firing through the open doorway, burning up their magazines without a clear target in sight. Levytsky left them to it, turning on his heel with a curt order to three other men, and raced back toward where he'd left the boss.

BOLAN HAD PAUSED deliberately on the final landing, well aware that gunfire in the stairwell would have roused the penthouse occupants, as well as any tenants on at least a couple of the floors below. He couldn't guess how many sleepy, frightened hands were clutching telephones and dialing 911, but after this night's bloody work, he knew police would be ready to roll, roughly a mile from the Ninth Precinct to Szold Place, maybe six minutes with their lights and sirens at that time of morning, with the traffic thinner than it ever was in prime time.

Still he waited, knowing that a leap beyond the fire door, into waiting guns, was tantamount to suicide.

It didn't take the shooters long to get their marching orders. Bolan couldn't see them, but he heard them coming. When the knob turned, he was ready, crouched below the line of sight for any man of average size. He glimpsed one scowling face and put a bullet through it, followed with a kick that slammed the heavy metal door back into two more men and sent them reeling from the impact, struggling to keep their balance. That was hopeless as he shot them both, a single round for each that sent them sprawling, then brushed past the door in search of other targets.

Two were facing him with submachine guns, others running down the short hallway, escaping toward the penthouse entrance. Bolan dropped and rolled, the rounds from their SMGs rattling the door behind him, ripping through its outer layer, then dropping down into the hollow core designed to offer three hours' protection against raging flames.

Bolan started rapid-firing when he hit the floor, still rolling, thankful that the soldiers hadn't bothered donning Kevlar. They skittered through a jerky little dance, one crumpling to his knees, the other toppling over backward, triggering a last long burst into the hallway's thin acoustic ceiling panels.

Still on the floor, Bolan squeezed off a parting shot at the retreating soldiers, nailed one in the lower back, and sent him sprawling as the others cleared the penthouse entryway and slammed the door behind them. When he rose and moved in that direction, the last guy he'd clipped was moaning, mouthing words that had to be profanity, and straining to retrieve a TEC-9 stuttergun he'd dropped when he went down.

It was beyond his reach, and since his legs no longer functioned, he was getting nowhere fast. Bolan relieved him of frustration with a mercy round through the head and turned to face the door that shielded Stepan Melnyk and the last of his defenders.

Mounted over it, a CCTV camera peered at Bolan from on high. He took it out with one more round, blinding his enemies inside the high-rise pad, and thought about the problem that confronted him.

His time was running out. Police would soon be on the scene in force, and he could only guess how many guns were waiting for him in the penthouse proper. Not the bravest thugs in town, the way they'd turned and bolted while their comrades died, but they would fight like any other cornered rats when it came down to that.

The only thing that Bolan had on his side now was shock and awe.

"What the hell's he waiting for?" Melnyk asked no one in particular.

"Maybe they got him," someone answered.

"Bullshit! Don't you think they'd tell us, so we could get out of here before the police show?"

"Maybe they got each other," someone else suggested.

"Great," Melnyk replied. "Why don't you go out there and check?"

"Well, I—"

"It's not a question! I said—"

But before he could repeat the order, Melnyk had to duck and cover, as rapid-firing shotgun blasts began to rip the place apart. They punched holes in the wall the size of dinner plates, six feet or so apart, spraying the room with buckshot, shattered wood and drywall as his men ducked and scurried for whatever cover they could find.

Melnyk himself was busy scrambling, so he didn't count the blasts. What difference did it make? The place was trashed already, his damage deposit shot all to hell, and all he could think of was finding a safe place to hide. The best he could do was a sectional sofa, twelve feet of leather and heavy construction, but the furthest thing on Earth from being bulletproof.

Diving across the sofa's back, he landed on Dimo Levytsky, there ahead of him, and drove the wind out of his chief lieutenant's lungs. Melnyk rolled off his gasping second in command and sneered at him. "Seems like what you're really good at in a fight is running, Dimo."

"Hey, Boss, I—"

"Shut up and help the others stop this son of a bitch before he kills us all!"

"Okay. Sure thing."

Levytsky was rising when a final shotgun blast took out the door. There was no way that Melnyk could mistake the sound of its wood splintering. From where he lay, he couldn't see his enemy approaching, but the shotgun switched off for some military-rifle *pop-pop-popping* at his men while they fired back, some of them crying out as they were hit.

Melnyk's second in command had recoiled when the door blew inward, quailing in the face of close-range hostile fire, but his boss wasn't letting him get off that easily. He jammed his pistol under his lieutenant's jaw, grinding the muzzle into him and gritted, "If you want to hide, you're no damn good to me. Get up and fight, or say g'bye right now."

"I'm going, Boss. I just—"

A sharp blow with the pistol shut him up and got him moving, scrabbling along the sofa's length on hands and knees, calling in Ukrainian to the others as he went. One of the soldiers who had answered Levytsky's call sped past him, ran into a bullet, did a little stutter step and fell beside Melnyk, his MP-5 creasing the godfather's scalp as it dropped. Melynk fired off a blue streak of curses, then clutched at the weapon with one hand, the other stuffing his pistol back under his belt.

Better.

If nothing else, at least now he could try to take some of his faceless adversaries with him when he died.

BOLAN WISHED HE had grenades, but he was making do with what he had. Clearing the penthouse doorway, once he'd blown it open with a round from his 12-gauge, Bolan dropped the Remington and switched back to the Colt AR-15. He'd swapped out magazines before he started using buckshot on the walls, ditching one partly empty mag in favor of a full 30-round load. It would be smarter, safer, he'd decided, than reloading in the midst of close combat, when cover might be sparse to nonexistent.

And somehow, against all odds, it seemed that he had caught them unprepared.

The hostiles knew that he was closing in, but watching as half a dozen of their comrades died, combined with the barrage of shotgun fire, had clearly dulled whatever fighting edge they'd once possessed. Only one soldier waited for him in the parlor, on his feet, wearing a battle face, and even he was slow enough that Bolan dropped him with a double-tap before he managed to get off a single shot.

That broke the spell, though, and another six or seven weapons opened up at once, all firing blind from cover in the living room or thrust around the corner of a doorway leading to the kitchen. Bullets drilled the walls and ceiling, shattered lamps and sent expensive-looking artwork tumbling to the floor.

So far, no lucky hits.

Bolan dived toward a massive recliner, rolled on past it as a couple of his adversaries sighted in. The Executioner came out on the other side, marking their forms and muzzle flashes, putting down two more. He couldn't say if they were dead or only wounded, but the way they'd fallen told him they were out of action for a while, at least.

Motion was life, and Bolan kept it going, rolling past the recliner to a heavy wooden coffee table, flipping it onto one edge and wriggling in behind it as a burst of Parabellum rounds came close enough to pepper him with splinters of mahogany. They stung, but didn't slow him as Bolan drew the Glock from shoulder leather with his left hand, awkward but still doable while clinging to the AR-15 with his right.

Time for another round of shock and awe.

He burst from cover, firing both weapons simultaneously, taking down a pair of shooters who had ceded common sense to wishful thinking, leaving cover prematurely. Next, he saw Dimo Levytsky rising with an MP-5K submachine gun, cracked his Adam's apple with a .40 S&W round and watched him drop back out of sight behind a massive sofa.

Two guys came for Bolan from the kitchen, firing as they ran, forgetting that it always helped to aim. He clipped them both and saw them fall together, one atop the other as they hit the floor and stayed there.

Sudden silence settled on the penthouse. Bolan didn't trust it, hadn't found the boss man yet, so he kept moving, circling gingerly around the long sofa that was the parlor's centerpiece. Three men were huddled on the floor back there, but only one of them was breathing now.

"It's over, Melnyk," Bolan told the godfather. "You want to stand up like a man or go out on your knees?"

"Smart bastard," Melnyk grumbled, struggling to his feet, his back still turned to Bolan, obviously trying to conceal some weapon clutched against his abdomen.

So Bolan shot him in the back with the Glock, low down. A submachine gun clattered to the floor, while Melnyk slumped against the sofa, yelling out his pain. Then suddenly it seemed that he was weeping.

"Smart guy," he rasped.

"One of us is," Bolan replied. "I have a question for you. Who's your contact in Kiev?"

"Go to hell!" Melnyk spit back at him.

"You first. You'll bleed out before the paramedics arrive," Bolan said.

Downstairs, still two or three blocks out, a siren wailed.

The Executioner dropped the AR-15 where he stood, holstered the Glock and headed for the stairs.

7

From the East Village, Bolan zigzagged through Manhattan, heading to JFK International Airport. The trip was sixteen miles and change, which translated to twenty-seven minutes on the road at 1:30 a.m.

With ample time to kill, he drove around the airport's long-term parking lot, disposing of the Glock and shoulder rig. He stripped the weapon, dropped its magazine in one trash can, its slide and barrel in another, grip and trigger assembly into a third, and holster in a fourth, before proceeding to the drop lot for his rental company. Once there, he slipped his keys and contract through a mail slot in the door—nobody working in the office at that hour—and began his long stroll to the terminal.

At that hour of the morning, JFK was relatively quiet. Most airlines wouldn't start selling tickets until 5:00 a.m., but Bolan had eliminated the middleman, going online from a Starbucks coffee shop parking lot to arrange his itinerary while police were still picking over remains of Stepan Melnyk's crew and wondering who'd put them down.

The State Department's website carried travel warnings for Ukraine, advising all Americans to stay away if they were not required to visit on some vital errand. No tourist visa was required for visits lasting less than ninety days, so he was clear on paperwork. As far as money went, foreigners were required to declare any bankrolls of ten thousand euros or more, but Bolan trusted the false bottom in his suitcase, shielded against X-rays, to conceal most of the stash he'd picked up in New York.

He required no paper ticket, having booked online, so he proceeded to his departure gate after he stopped to buy two newspapers along the way.

His exploits hadn't hit the *New York Times* yet, a lapse for the city's "newspaper of record." The *New York Post* was doing better, in its garish tabloid style, with photos of the previous afternoon's crime scenes, but was still playing catch-up with the final denouement in Brighton Beach and the East Village.

As a rule, Bolan had little interest in the spin reporters put on anything he did. Most of his foreign missions never got a mention in the States, while those that caused a stir were normally attributed to conflict between rebel groups, criminal elements, whatever. While he craved no personal publicity, far from it, he was frequently amazed at the degree of ignorance and apathy his fellow citizens displayed toward world events and groups that threatened their security.

What had the country come to, when politicians in the national arena spoke of Africa as "a country," confused Islamic radicals with "communists" or closed their eyes to the perils and promise of modern science? When everyone was angry about something, but two-thirds of them were too lazy to spend five minutes voting every other year, what lay in store for the United States?

These moods came over him from time to time, but lasted momentarily. This morning, waiting for a flight halfway around the world to yet another combat zone, he shook it off as always, focused on his mission of the moment, and determined that he'd give it everything he had.

It was the only way Mack Bolan knew to play the game.

Kiev, Ukraine

PAVLO VOLOSHYN TOOK the bad news as he always did, in silence, with his face deadpan. No casual observer would have guessed that he was raging on the inside as he listened to the caller from Manhattan, visualizing scenes of carnage that would put most slasher films to shame.

Some of the scenes his mind played out were memories; the others, wishful plans.

"I understand," Voloshyn said, when he had heard it all. "Keep me updated if you learn more, absolutely. Use whatever cash you have on hand for funeral arrangements. And do nothing with the property until you hear from me."

It was the best that he could do from where he sat in his office near the ancient Golden Gate, overlooking the Dnieper River. He had lawyers and accountants to concern themselves with such details, one of the top firms in Manhattan on retainer for a sum that would have made him blanch ten years ago. Of course, Voloshyn had not been a warlord then.

How times had changed.

There had been times when Voloshyn hadn't believed he would live to reach his forty-first birthday, now six months behind him, and others when he'd been convinced that he would finish out his days in prison. He'd been wrong on both counts, thanks in equal part to personal determination, ruthlessness and Russian meddling in his homeland. He had been born a Russian subject, liberated with his country when the Soviet Union dissolved in 1991, but now the bear was back again, snuffling around and claiming territory for itself, provoking what amounted to a civil war among his countrymen.

Voloshyn could admit it to himself, however—war was good for business in so many ways. It helped divert authorities from routes where contraband was smuggled and increased his profits from the arms trade. Refugees, particularly young women and children, were ideal targets for human trafficking—no families to miss them, no real inclination by police to learn where they had gone, if anyone even remembered they existed.

In his role as a supporter of Ukraine's resistance against Moscow, Voloshyn had gained a measure of respectability and influence that had eluded him throughout his adult life. He was a folk hero to some; to others, a figure feared and admired in equal measure.

Not that he regarded *all* Russians as enemies, by any means. Voloshyn could honestly say that some of his best friends were Russian—not members of the current leader's regime, but still close to the true seat of power, oligarchs and cartel leaders who were not political in any normal sense but who survived and prospered from relations with the government, subverting it occasionally, more often collaborating with it, buying portions of it when the price was right.

Now, with the bad news from Manhattan on his plate, he owed one of his Russian friends a call. With any luck, Voloshyn could prevent a rift, forestall the outbreak of another costly war.

And if he failed…well, there was something to be said for striking first.

Mid-Atlantic, 40,000 feet altitude

THE UIA AIRLINER'S menu offered travelers a choice of meals. One was a "full course" dinner, featuring salad, a

hot entrée and dessert; the other was a "testy" Caesar sandwich. Bolan gambled on a typo in that case and chose the
sandwich, with a beer to wash it down, knowing he still
had six full hours of airtime yet ahead of him. The food
was fine, not irritable in the least, and when he'd finished
it, he pulled the plastic shade down on his window and relaxed with sleep in mind.

Despite his long experience at sleeping anywhere and
everywhere, as time allowed, the dark oblivion eluded him
at first. His mind was focused on Kiev and on what was
waiting for him there.

Ukraine's capital lay outside the troubled country's
major war zone, which was farther to the east in Donbass,
on the Russian border. Still, the impact of that fighting had
been felt in countless ways, including acts of terrorism, dis-
placed persons streaming westward, protest demonstrations
on both sides of Russian annexation and challenges from
Chechen paramilitaries who regarded Ukraine's lawfully
elected government as an oppressive junta suppressing the
will of the people.

Nothing new in that, per se, for a society whose national
anthem was titled "Ukraine Has Not Yet Died." Most of
it lay beyond Bolan's brief for this mission—"above his
pay grade," in the popular smart-ass lingo. What *did* concern him was the rise in crime throughout Ukraine, particularly organized varieties, including but by no means
limited to narco-trafficking, gunrunning and wholesale
human trafficking.

As Brognola's dossier had informed him, the top ranks
of Ukrainian organized crime included native-born mobsters, interloping Russians and Chechens, plus stragglers
from Poland, Albania, Romania and the Czech Republic
fighting for scraps from the big boys' table. Two leaders in
particular stood out from Brognola's synopsis, one for his

presumed ties to Stepan Melnyk in New York, the other a Russian who played both sides in Ukraine's civil war, arming the Right Front and various other half-baked militias with the tools to kill one another and an untold number of civilians, using the chaos of wartime to cover his traffic in contraband flowing both ways through Ukraine.

The first was Pavlo Voloshyn, a thug with more cunning than most of his cronies so far, who'd started out peddling drugs on street corners, graduated to booking bets, then fixing soccer matches to improve his odds, then to loansharking and smuggling of all kinds. Authorities suspected that he'd killed his first man at the tender age of nineteen years, but they could never prove that case—or any of the twenty-seven others logged against his name in "open" files. Voloshyn had served time for pimping and possession of narcotics, the latter overturned when the state's key witness begged to recant his original testimony. Not that it helped him: he had disappeared, shortly after Voloshyn walked out of prison a free man.

Stepan Melnyk had been a middle-ranking cog in Voloshyn's machine when he served a short term of his own, for assault, and then decided to try his luck in New York. NSA logs and other sources revealed ongoing communication between Melnyk and two numbers in Kiev that traced back to businesses owned by Voloshyn. No one could prove the two men personally spoke, but Bolan wasn't laying out a case for trial. He operated from experience, gut instinct and the kind of common sense too many people had forgotten in an age of social media, where every passing thought was posted to the web and viewed by thousands—sometimes millions—in the course of hours.

In every way that mattered, he *knew* that Melnyk and Voloshyn were connected. Whether it had been a sometime partnership of pure convenience, or some kind of master-servant operation, Bolan neither knew nor cared.

The Russian angle in Kiev was more or less controlled by Bogdan Britnev, forty-eight, a native of St. Petersburg who'd moved to Moscow as a child and prospered there after the fall of communism ushered in a kind of chaos. He had followed all the normal steps from street muscle to leadership among the criminal element, then saw a golden opportunity in Ukraine with the outbreak of war and set up a branch office there. According to the goods from Stony Man, he worked closely with Voloshyn, although they'd also had their spats from time to time.

That's interesting, Bolan thought, before he drifted off, at last, to dreamless sleep.

Kiev, Ukraine

"I HEARD ABOUT your comrade's difficulty in New York," Bogdan Britnev said, frowning at the speakerphone in front of him. "My friends also have had some…difficulties."

"Coincidence, you think?" his caller asked.

"It's always possible," Britnev allowed. "But likely? I am skeptical."

"As I am," Pavlo Voloshyn replied.

"The problem with such things is—"

"Distance," Voloshyn finished for him.

"Exactly. I have other people in the neighborhood who could investigate, perhaps, but do I risk them? Is it easier and wiser just to wait and see what happens next?"

"That's why I'm calling."

"Ah." Now they were getting to the crux of it.

"I have received a message from Manhattan. One of Melnyk's people. Did you ever meet Stepan?"

"I never had the pleasure," Britnev said.

"I wouldn't go that far, but he was competent—or so I thought."

"The message?" Britnev prodded him.

"From one of the survivors."

"Naturally." How could dead men make a trans-Atlantic call?

"He thought one man, or possibly a small group, might have been responsible for what befell my friends, and yours."

Britnev considered that. "Official?" he inquired.

"There was no indication of it. No arrests until the bodies started falling. Only now are members of the FBI beginning to investigate."

"A covert agency, perhaps?" Britnev suggested.

"If it had happened here," Voloshyn said, "I might suspect the police. Americans, for the most part, only behave that way in other countries, I believe."

"But now, you think…?"

"I'm not sure. If there was a motive…"

"Something like the incident in Washington, perhaps?"

"That was not my affair!"

"Of course. I understand." Britnev smiled at the speakerphone. "But it could easily be misinterpreted."

"In which case, why attack your interests, as well?" Voloshyn asked.

And that *was* troubling. It suggested knowledge no one should possess. "I have no answer," Britnev finally admitted.

"Then, I think we both should be on guard."

"Here? In Kiev?"

"Until we know there is no danger from outside," Voloshyn said.

Stating the obvious, Britnev replied, "I am always on guard."

"But more than normal, eh? Until this passes, or we manage to explain it."

Britnev tried to see the angles, figure out how Voloshyn's alarmism could injure him, but saw nothing. "There's never any harm in being cautious," he agreed.

"And we should stay in touch."

"As usual, comrade."

"Good day, then."

"And to you."

Britnev switched off the speakerphone and rocked back in his chair, scowled at the vaulted ceiling of his office for a while, and then reached out to make the first of several urgent calls.

Boryspil International Airport, Kiev, Ukraine

BOLAN'S FLIGHT WAS seven minutes early, which impressed him. He collected his single suitcase from the baggage claim area, then proceeded to Customs and Immigration, presenting the young, fresh-faced clerk with a passport in the name of Matthew Cooper, with a New York address. He claimed tourism as the reason for his visit, verified that he would leave the country before ninety days and said that he had nothing to declare. The kid seemed to consider opening his bags, then let it go and stamped his passport with a green-ink rectangular seal, including the date and some text Bolan couldn't translate.

He had booked a car while he was somewhere over the Atlantic, reserving a ZAZ Vida four-door sedan from Sixt at the airport.

His Amex Platinum card—again, under Matt Cooper's name—secured the ride and all available insurance, just in case. He paid extra for GPS to help him navigate, and programmed it for English once he'd found the Vida parked outside and done a walk-around to satisfy himself that it was fit for service.

Bolan's list of local contacts, courtesy of Stony Man, was short: two arms dealers who sometimes did work for the CIA, and an officer of the Ukrainian National Police who had collaborated with the DEA and FBI on cases where his own brass turned blind eyes to flagrant criminal activities. That contact was a corporal who had poor prospects for longevity, much less advancement, if he held his present course.

Good news for Bolan in a pinch, but not so much for Corporal Maksym Sushko, if he delved too deeply into Bolan's war.

The arms dealers were simpler, strictly play for pay without a thought as to what their products might be used for. One operated in Kiev's Darnytsia District, on the city's southeast side, the other downtown, in Pechersk. He chose the second, for proximity to Kiev International, and programmed the address into his GPS before he left the airport's parking lot. A mellow voice, androgynous yet somehow pleasing, steered him toward his destination, offering encouragement and guidance all the way.

He found the address he was looking for on Naddnipryans'ke Highway, on the left bank of the Dnieper River. Proprietor Itzik Franko ran a hair salon, catering to stylish clients who had no idea that underneath the sinks where they were shampooed and the chairs where they were blow-dried lay a basement filled with lethal military wares.

It took longer to park near Franko's shop than to cross town and find the place, but Bolan got it done. He locked the ZAZ and walked a block back to his destination, wondering how he would lug his purchases along the crowded sidewalk in broad daylight, unobserved.

One problem at a time.

He reached the shop, peered through its window at a row of women sitting under hair driers resembling old-time space helmets and pushed his way inside.

8

Bykivnia, Kiev

Bolan crossed the Dnieper River to meet his contact in a city of the dead. Bykivnia, situated in Kiev's northeastern quadrant on the Chernihiv Highway, had been a thriving village until Josef Stalin's paranoia overwhelmed him in the mid-1930s, prompting the Great Purge that included winnowing of real and imaginary traitors from the Red Army and Communist Party, coupled with repression of rural peasants. First hundreds, then thousands and tens of thousands vanished into prisons or forced labor camps, and from there to mass graves.

One such repository for "the disappeared" was now a National Historic Memorial, the Bykivnia Graves. Most of its modern, silent occupants began their journey to Bykivnia at Lukyanivska Prison, built for 2,800 inmates and commonly jam-packed with twice that many until not-so-secret executions started up in 1936, serving the function of a steam pressure release valve. Meanwhile, at Bykivnia, mass burials first frightened off, then crowded out the living residents, until the town became a grim Ukrainian necropolis.

Graveyards didn't bother Bolan. Generally, they made nice, quiet meeting places with long lines of sight. He'd met often with Hal Brognola at Arlington National Cemetery, outside DC, and sometimes visited that resting place of heroes even when he wasn't on a job for Stony Man.

Bolan had no fear of the dead, friendly or otherwise, and if the living caused a problem for him at Bykivnia, he would be prepared.

His shopping at the Franko hair salon had worked out well. For his primary weapon, Bolan had purchased an AK-12 assault rifle, a modern version of the classic Kalashnikov, chambered in 5.45 mm, featuring a red dot scope and laser sight; a telescoping in-line stock for better recoil control; an ambidextrous cocking lever and fire selector, the latter offering semi-auto, 3-round bursts, and full-auto fire at a top rate of six hundred rounds per minute, or a thousand rpm when set in 3-round-burst mode.

For distance work he had a Turkish Kalekalip-Tubitak KNT-308 bolt-action sniper's rifle, chambered in 7.62 mm and mounting a Steiner 5-25x scope with a G2B Mil-Dot illuminated reticle, including a four-post crosshair configuration. His sidearm was a Glock 18 selective fire pistol, muzzle threaded to accept a suppressor, and he'd backed that up with a Russian NR-40 combat knife boasting a black wooden handle, an S-shaped guard and a six-inch clip point blade.

Finally, in case he had to replicate the big bang theory, Bolan had picked up an RPG-7 with a variety of rockets, and supplemented that with a dozen F1 hand grenades of Russian manufacture.

So Bolan was ready for anything short of an air strike as he approached the Bykivnia Graves, parked the ZAZ and prepared to go EVA. He was supposed to meet his contact at a monument set in woodland, constructed like a huge rock cairn, surmounted by nine stylized concrete crosses. Bolan already had it spotted, with a cheap tourist map for backup, and made his way toward it on foot.

The only question now: would he be meeting with a live contact, or adding to the local population of ghosts?

CORPORAL MAKSYM SUSHKO parked his unmarked Mitsubishi Lancer north of the Bykivnia Graves and walked back for his rendezvous with a stranger. The solid weight of his Fort-12 double-action pistol, cocked and locked with thirteen rounds of 9 mm ammunition, was reassuring to a point, but as he neared his destination under gray skies, with a rising wind, Sushko wished he had brought the AKSU-74 SMG from his car.

Should he go back for it?

Not now. It would betray weakness, if anyone was watching him, and enemies already hidden in the cemetery were more likely to attack him when his back was turned.

Sushko trusted the contact who had sent him here, but only to a point. Full trust in anyone, these days, was very difficult to nurture, even harder to maintain. He served in the National Police under Ukraine's Ministry of Internal Affairs. Times were changing, but brutality and corruption still existed. However, Sushko knew many officers who did their best with what they had, trying to fight crime and preserve the peace.

And he was one of them.

What brought him here, then, meeting with a foreigner in what his superiors would likely call an act of treason?

Corporal Sushko was fed up, disgusted by the negligence and corruption that still existed in the newly formed National Police. Winnowing out the old guard was not happening as quickly as the government had planned. He felt embarrassed by association with the officers who sold themselves to oligarchs and mobsters, turning into errand boys, bagmen, muscle and even executioners for those they should have been arresting and sending off to prison in chains. His government had repealed capital punishment in 2000, to wangle a seat on the Council of Europe, and while Sushko recognized the many abuses of execution under both Russian and post-Soviet rule, he still believed that some people needed to die.

Child traffickers were one example. Every time he heard about another case, he wished the perpetrators dead and roasting in a hell whose existence he had long ago abandoned as a childish fantasy. And when a prosecution failed because some officer was paid to lose the crucial evidence, Sushko added a fresh name to his list.

His contact, the freckle-faced American who smiled too much and chuckled at his own jokes, had told Sushko that the man he would be meeting here, among the dead, was "serious"—someone adept at solving problems so that they did not recur tomorrow, next week or next year. His interest, of course, was in the spillage of Ukrainian mayhem into the United States, highlighted by the recent incident in Washington.

No one, it seemed, cared about Ukraine for Ukraine alone.

No one, perhaps, but Sushko. *He* cared, and so he would listen to this foreigner, perhaps cooperate if there was something in it for his homeland and himself. If the proposal put him off, he would refuse. If that, in turn, angered the would-be comic who had paid him the princely sum of one hundred dollars per week for the past eighteen months, then so be it. Sushko was content to live without the extra money and the interference in his life.

And if the freckled-faced American tried to blackmail

him somehow…well, there were ways to deal with that, as well.

Sushko could see his landmark now, the rising cairn and crosses, still roughly one hundred yards away. He scanned the graveyard, spotting isolated mourners here and there, stray groups of morbid tourists passing through.

He pushed on, looking for the stranger who might change—or end—his life.

"HURRY UP!" VASYL KYRYLOVYCH SAID. "We're losing him!"

"We're losing nobody," Roman Cherkassky replied. "If we get too close, we'll put him on alert."

"I don't like this," Emil Staryk chimed in. "It's all too open and exposed."

"Meaning you're too fat," Cherkassky said. "No one asked you if you like it."

"No, but—"

"Pay attention. Watch our man."

Another three-man team was trailing the policeman at a distance, moving in parallel. Cherkassky didn't understand why this man should rate six watchers. He knew the corporal had been snooping where he shouldn't, stepping on some tender toes, but that was reason to eliminate him, not waste time and manpower trailing him around Kiev indefinitely. Every day he lived created new risks of exposure.

Why not simply kill him here and now?

Because Cherkassky's orders were explicit: *Find out who he's meeting.*

Then, and only then, could he eliminate the corporal and snatch his contact for interrogation, find out who he was, how much he knew, what information had been traded off between them.

Cherkassky thought he was prepared for anything. All six men on the job were well armed and proficient with the weapons they'd selected. All of them were killers, not a breed particularly scarce around Ukraine these days. When Cherkassky gave the order, they would act efficiently, accepting any consequences from return fire. If the corporal resisted, or if more policemen appeared, the team would deal with them.

They hung well back, two hundred yards at least, trailing the cop. Cherkassky had not known where he was going, but the target made it obvious, beelining for the great cairn with its crosses, seeming heedless of the other graves around him. In the farther distance, well beyond the cairn, Cherkassky's eyes picked out more idlers in the boneyard. Any one of them could be the person whom the corporal had come to meet—or any pair, for that matter, although he paid scant attention to the stooped and elderly.

The corporal would not have come to meet some doddering grandmother at this monument to death, and what could some old lady know in any case? Cherkassky looked for someone who could pose a threat to the organization he served, if not a man, at least a woman who was young and fit enough to hold a station of responsibility.

But what if this were something else? What if the corporal was on some private errand best conducted secretly, feeding some vice of which he was ashamed? It was entirely possible, Cherkassky thought. No one was perfect, and the ones who thought they were most often proved to be the greatest hypocrites of all.

Cherkassky spoke into his Bluetooth headset. "Team two, you see anything?"

The answer came back loud and clear. "Nothing yet."

"Okay. Keep your eyes sharp."

"Why don't we just *kill* him?" Staryk asked. "That settles everything."

"You want to tell the boss that, when we come back empty-handed?" Cherkassky asked.

"It's not my job," the shooter answered petulantly.

"And it's not your job to think up bright ideas, either. So keep them to yourself."

"Yeah, yeah. Okay."

Cherkassky fidgeted, feeling the PP-2000 submachine gun underneath his raincoat, on its shoulder sling, rubbing against his ribs. He would be glad to use it when the time came, but for now they had to watch and wait.

One target was not good enough. Cherkassky absolutely needed two.

BOLAN WAS LOITERING behind the massive cairn when he saw a lone figure approaching. The man wore a knee-length trench coat, trudging along with his hands buried deep in the coat's outer pockets. A fedora that had witnessed better days sat squarely on his head, its snap brim pulled down nearly to his eyebrows.

That coat could hide a mini-arsenal, as Bolan's raincoat did. He couldn't blame Corporal Sushko from anticipating trouble at their rendezvous, but first he needed to confirm that this *was* Maksym Sushko in the flesh, and not some ringer sent to bait a trap. The face half shadowed by the old fedora *might* be Sushko's at a hundred yards, but Bolan would require a closer look to match against the photographs he'd memorized from Hal Brognola's file.

At fifty yards his doubts began to ease, but Bolan kept his right hand wrapped around the pistol grip of his assault rifle, accessible through the raincoat's slit pocket, designed for reaching keys and cash during a downpour, but as useful now for self-defense.

At thirty yards the cop lifted his head, and Bolan verified that it was his contact. It was a long face, with a mournful cast, as if Sushko had witnessed too much misery, internalized it, until it was leaking from his eyes. It was a look Bolan had seen on many law-enforcement officers around the world, and as strange as it might sound, it made him hopeful.

Bad cops, in his personal experience, showed little on their faces beyond arrogance. They simply didn't care.

"Corporal Sushko," Bolan said, when they were close enough to speak without raising their voices. He released the AK-12, offered his hand and introduced himself. "Matt Cooper."

Sushko's upper lip twitched slightly, either from a nervous tic or logging the false information and dismissing it. If he had any sense at all, he'd know that Bolan wasn't handing out his true name to a stranger he'd met for the first time in a Ukrainian graveyard.

"Shall we complete the ritual?" Sushko asked.

"Might as well," Bolan agreed, and launched into the prearranged pass phrase. "It is good fishing—"

"—in streamy water." Sushko finished the Ukrainian proverb, signifying that people may take advantage of chaos to gain their own ends.

"This must seem odd to you," Bolan allowed.

"Life frequently seems odd to me, these days," Sushko replied.

"If you have any qualms…"

"None." Sushko fanned the air as if swatting at gnats. "I need help. My country needs help."

"I'm just one man, you understand," Bolan said. "No one else is coming. If we take this road—"

"It may be the end of us. I understand completely."

"I'm hoping not. But, yes. Are you good with that?"

"I have no family except a sister whom I rarely see, only this job which, often, I am not allowed to do because it might upset someone who ought to be in prison or a coffin. *Da*, I am ready."

"Okay, then. We should—"

Movement out among the graves caught Bolan's eye, just a peripheral until he turned in that direction and the flicker became three men moving closer to the cairn, two hundred yards and closing. The cairn obscured his vision to the left, but Bolan saw one of the new arrivals glance in that direction, lifting one hand in a signal to somebody off in that direction.

"Is this a setup?" he asked Sushko, as his AK-12 eased out from under cover.

"What?"

"Three men at two o'clock. More that I can't see on the far side of the cairn."

The corporal began to turn, but Bolan stopped him with a terse "Stand still."

"They must have followed me. It was clumsy of me. I am sorry."

Bolan judged him in two seconds flat and thought he was sincere, whatever that was worth. A careless partner was the next-worst thing, in Bolan's estimation, to a traitor at his side.

"If these are other cops—"

The corporal shook his head emphatically. "No one from the office knows where I am. Of that, I'm sure."

"Okay. We need to clean this up," Bolan declared. "It would be nice if we could grab one of these guys and question him, but I'm not counting on it. Step one is to stay alive and mobile. Are you packing?"

Sushko frowned at him, not understanding.

"Armed," Bolan translated.

"*Da*. A pistol only, with me. In my car I have—"

"Nothing that's any use to us right now. How many rounds?"

"Three magazines make thirty-six plus one."

"All right, then. Make them count," Bolan replied. "Now follow me."

"I'VE LOST THEM. They have passed behind the cairn," Roman Cherkassky said into his Bluetooth microphone. "Do you have any visual?"

Stas Hutz replied, voice small and peevish in Cherkassy's ear. "Nothing from here."

"Move in!" Cherkassky snapped. "They could be running."

Hutz answered with a curse and passed the order on.

Cherkassky saw the second team advancing quickly toward the cairn and wondered if they might already be too late.

This was supposed to be an easy snatch and grab, but if it turned into a running fight through the Bykivnia Graves it could easily get out of hand. Cherkassky didn't know the stats offhand, but if he had to guess, he would have said the graveyard sprawled over at least 140 acres. Hiking in, he had already passed at least two dozen witnesses who ordinarily would not have noticed his small party, but if there was shooting in this solemn place—

The first crack was a pistol shot, followed immediately by another curse from Hutz's side. "Damn! I almost had him!"

"Who told you to fire?" Cherkassky challenged him.

"I thought—"

"Don't think!" Cherkassky snarled back. "What about the other one?"

"No sight of him. I think—"

This time there was a buzz of automatic fire, two bursts

from what Cherkassky took to be a Kalashnikov, one of
the smaller, newer calibers. Glancing to his right, he saw
the backup team diving for cover where there wasn't much
but headstones, belly-down in grass that left them open for
the most part, scared to lift their heads and look for targets.

"Jesus!" Turning to his grim comrades, Cherkassky said,
"Come on. We have to help them out before this blows up
in our faces and we all go down the toilet."

"Kill the pair of them," Staryk suggested. "Easy."

"Screw trying to take one back alive," Kyrylovych
added.

They had a point, but there was still the boss, their godfather, to think about. When Pavlo Voloshyn gave orders,
he did not expect to have them modified, much less ignored
completely. Disappointing him was much the same as bending down to kiss a hungry crocodile. Your drunken friends
might be impressed at first, but that would be no consola-
tion when the reptile tore you limb from limb.

"Follow my lead exactly," he instructed his teammates.
"No deviations, or you can explain them to the godfather
yourself."

That said, clutching his SMG, Cherkassky ran to join
the fight.

CAUTIOUS ANNIHILATION, BOLAN had decided, was the way to
go. He hadn't counted on a showdown at his first meeting
with Sushko, but the fat was in the fire now and he couldn't
alter that. The first shot, fired without a warning, put his
mind at ease about the stalkers being cops, but there were
still civilians in the neighborhood, which argued against
pulling out the stops and hitting them with everything he
had, grenades and all.

But that didn't mean they got to walk away.

The first burst from Bolan's AK-12 had been to keep

their heads down. They had a pincers movement going, working on encirclement, and Bolan only knew two ways to counter that: withdraw or claim the high ground for himself.

He guessed the hunters would expect him to retreat, a logical enough assumption when outnumbered three to one. That might have been the way to go, if he were a civilian or a cop armed only with a pistol, hedged around by rules and regulations, but the shooters had unwittingly surprised another kind of animal entirely when they sprang their trap. This prey was strong, ferocious on a level they had likely never seen before, and well prepared to fight.

"What should I do?" asked Sushov, cutting into Bolan's thoughts.

"Head west and draw their fire. Not far. Just buy me time to get up high."

Sushko glanced toward the concrete crosses on the cairn. "You fight up there?"

"It's cover," Bolan said. "The dead don't mind."

"And I just run away?"

"Not far, I said. You're bait. Distract them."

"Bait," Sushov repeated, then translated it into Ukrainian. "*Prymanka*. As you wish." He had a pistol in his right hand now, the hammer cocked.

"One more thing," Bolan told him. "Don't get killed."

Sushko managed a thin, anemic smile at that. "I'll do my best," he said, and turned away.

Bolan was climbing by the time the corporal hit his stride, trusting the peaked mound of the cairn to cover his ascent as long as he stayed low and didn't start a rock slide to betray himself.

In fact, the stones were more like granite blocks, broken and piled to form a mound approximately twenty feet in height, surmounted by the concrete crosses shown on post cards and in countless tourist photographs. This was no grassy knoll, ideal for sniping from. If lying prone, the blocks would gouge his ribs, scrape knees and elbows, bruise his flesh, but all of that was better than a bullet to the head. Rough ground was nothing new to Bolan, and he wouldn't let it stop him now.

Climbing, the AK-12 clutched tight against his chest, he saw two teams, one on either side of him, observing Sushko, tracking him and waiting for another figure to appear. The six all had their weapons angled westward, scoping on their solitary target, holding fire until they figured out where number two had gone.

Bolan had nearly reached the summit, and he didn't plan to keep them waiting long.

9

Maksym Sushko felt as if he had been dropped into the middle of a fever dream from which there was no waking. First, he cursed himself for leaving his Kalashnikov back in the trunk of his patrol car, hopelessly beyond his reach now, then resolved himself to follow the American's instructions.

What choice did he have, in fact?

Sushko felt terribly exposed as he jogged westward from the cairn, his back turned toward the enemy, whose weapons could reach out and cut him down at any second. It ran counter to his training and experience, but he could understand the logic of it, drawing their attention while the man who called himself Matt Cooper went to work with his assault rifle.

But was he any good with it? Was anyone outside of Spetznaz or the Alpha Group of Ukraine's own Security Service prepared to fight six men at once? More to the point, what would become of Sushko if Cooper were killed? Cut off from his vehicle, barred from calling backup on his covert mission, how much longer would he stay alive?

A burst of automatic fire behind him made the corporal flinch, hunching his shoulders, but the bullets did not find him. Cooper had engaged the enemy, it seemed, and

they were firing back at him. It struck Sushko that he had
no idea who "they" were, how'd they'd trailed him to the
meeting, and the void in knowledge troubled him as much
as the idea of being hunted like an animal.

He had been hunted in the past, by gangsters and by terrorists. Sushko had beaten all of them so far—killed some,
jailed others—but at no time had he been in any doubt as
to the motive or identity of his would-be assassins. Now
he felt foolish, nearly helpless. Were the gunmen Russian
or Ukrainian? Was their desire to kill him motivated by
revenge, by politics, by greed?

More firing came from the cairn, and still no bullets
were fired his way. As bait, it seemed that he was worthless.
The American was pinned down on the cairn but fighting
back, surrounded. He had held his own so far, but no one
could defend every side at once. If Cooper died, the gunmen would be after Sushko in a heartbeat. If they captured
him alive and carried him away…

For starters, they'd be able to confirm Sushko's collaboration with a foreign government, unauthorized by his superiors. They could expose him as a traitor if it suited them,
leave his destruction to his fellow officers or to Ukraine's
Security Service. Who would believe that he simply intended to help his homeland and saw no way to do that
within the flawed system he served?

Perhaps a priest, if Sushko had believed in all that
mumbo-jumbo.

Someone cried out, high and sharp behind him, badly
wounded. Stopping in his tracks, he turned to face the cairn
but had no view of Cooper at its pinnacle. Was he already
down, wounded or dying?

Sushko cursed himself again, as seven kinds of idiot,
and ran back toward the fight.

BOLAN WASN'T DEAD or wounded, though his enemies had
done their best so far to put him down. Sporadic fire from
left and right, circling the cairn, had peppered him with
granite shards and splinters from the looming concrete
crosses, stinging slivers from the ricochets that missed
him, but the shooters hadn't tagged him yet.

From shot one of the battle, they were on the clock.
Bolan had passed enough civilians in the graveyard to assume that several—likely dozens—were aware of gun-
play in the cemetery. A guidebook he had studied while in
flight reported that three Ukrainian mobile phone networks
claimed fifty-eight million subscribers between them, not
bad for a country whose last census counted only forty-six
million inhabitants. The odds of someone calling the police, therefore, stood right around 100 percent.

That was good *and* bad news. If Bolan simply held his
ground until the cavalry arrived, his mission would be
scrubbed, his journey wasted. Sushko couldn't help him
without sacrificing his career, maybe his life, and disavowal
was a given when it came to Stony Man. So he would have
to clean this up, and in a hurry, if he wanted to get clear and
reconnect with Sushko somewhere down the line.

He had already dropped one of the hunters, with the first
burst from his AK-12, but they learned quickly from the
loss and played it cagey, moving close to the broad base of
the cairn. They might not have a shot at him from below,
that way, but physics hampered Bolan in the same way.
He'd be forced to stand, expose himself to gunmen on all
sides, if he began to thin the pack.

At least Sushko was clear, it seemed. None of the thugs
had followed him, which told Bolan the corporal was *a* target, not *the* target. Who would have known Sushko was
meeting someone at the cemetery, much less that he might
be meeting with a foreigner? He ruled out any kind of

leak from Stony Man. Most likely it was vague intel about a meet with no specifics, someone marking Sushko as a man to watch for causing trouble in the past and cultivating squealers, walking in on something that they didn't understand.

At least, he *hoped* that was the case, and there was no more time to ponder it.

Fight now. Think later.

He inched over jagged granite, nice to look at but a pain to crawl on, angling for a decent shot that wouldn't get him killed, when 9 mm pistol fire cracked out somewhere from the west side of the cairn. Bolan heard a flurry of presumed Ukrainian obscenities.

Sushko?

He didn't second-guess it, turning painfully on his bed of fractured stones and facing toward the battle sounds.

"STAS? ARE YOU THERE? Answer me, damn it!"

"He can't hear you," Taryk Korot told Cherkassky via Bluetooth. "Stas is gone."

"Useless prick!" Cherkassky spit back through his microphone. "Finished for good?"

"I saw his brains," Korot replied.

All right. When there was fighting, people died. That was the long and short of it. Cherkassky had been friends with Stas Hutz, but he was not about to let grief cripple him.

"Who has a clear shot at the shooter?" he asked both teams at once.

"None here," Korot said.

"Same for me," Nissan Bibik replied, and so it went around the circle, Kyrylovych and Staryk both confirming that they could not see the enemy from where they'd gone to ground.

"The only way to spot him," Staryk said, "means giving him a shot at one of us."

Cherkassky recognized the truth of it. He said, "That's it, then. Any volunteers?"

He half expected mocking laughter, but the silence from his earpiece said it all.

"I choose, then. Taryk, do it."

"Why me?" Korot challenged.

"Stas was your friend."

"Yours, too!"

"I never—"

Sudden pistol fire cut off his words, *pop-popping* from the west, Cherkassky's left.

"Who's firing, damn it?" he demanded. "If you can't—"

"The cop's back," Kyrylovych said. "He couldn't leave his boyfriend, after all."

More firing, answered by a burst from a Kalashnikov that failed to do the trick, since pistol shots immediately followed. From the far side of the cairn, a cry of pain wafted on dull breeze to Cherkassky's ears.

"Who's that?" he hissed into the Bluetooth. "Sound off if you hear me!"

"Vasyl here."

"Taryk."

"Nissan."

Cherkassky waited for the last voice for a moment, then barked, "Emil? Staryk? Answer!"

"Hit bad," Staryk answered finally, half choking on it. "Too much blood."

A spark of panic flared inside Cherkassky's chest then quickly smothered as he clenched his teeth and said, "Hold on. I'm coming for you."

"Roman, no!" Staryk replied. "You—"

Pop! Another pistol shot, undoubtedly 9 mm, slapped

at Cherkassky's eardrum. He recoiled, grimacing at the pain, feeling raw fury rise and threaten to eclipse coherent thought.

Cherkassky had already used at least two-thirds of his SMG's 20-round magazine, trying to bring down the man on the cairn's top. He pulled it now and stuffed it in a pocket, replacing the 20-round stick with a larger one, loaded with forty-four rounds. Four seconds of sustained fired would exhaust it, but if he could frame the target in his sights, Cherkassky would not mind.

Rage and frustration drove him as he started scuttling toward the sound of pistol fire.

ATOP THE CAIRN, Mack Bolan felt the tide of battle shift. Sushko's return had taken his opponents by surprise, and since it seemed the corporal had eliminated one of them, the four survivors were prepared to treat him as the more immediate and deadly threat.

Not wise—in fact, a foolish move—but Bolan was prepared to take advantage of it.

Ten yards, all jutting granite edges, separated Bolan from the east side of the cairn, where he would have to slide and scramble twenty feet or more downslope to plant his feet on level ground. The cairn had been surrounded seconds earlier, but he had tracked a shifting movement of his enemies westward as they rushed to cover Maksym Sushko on the other side. They might have left a man behind, on watch, but one was better than a four-man firing squad.

The Executioner reached the edge, peered over, hearing more gunshots and shouts behind him, and saw no one down below. That was a drawback of the cairn's curving perimeter, but if he planned to make the move it had to be right then.

And once he reached the ground below, should he go left or right?

Bolan decided he would take that as it came.

He started down the jagged slope, no shortage of footholds, no dearth of sharp edges to cut him and snag on his clothing. Gripping his Kalashnikov in one hand, balancing and bracing with the other, he descended one step at a time, scanning for enemies who might have doubled back, tense in anticipation of a tumbling fall.

He jumped the last ten feet and landed in a crouch, spun in a quick three-sixty with his AK-12 sweeping the ground in front of him, the vast expanse of graves beyond.

When no one challenged him immediately, Bolan circled to his left, around the longer north side of the cairn, one of its two long sides. He didn't rush it, homing in on the shouts of men who masked fear with profanity and anger.

Had they cornered Sushko yet? Was he already down? Had Bolan come too late to help the ally he had barely met?

A few more steps, and Bolan saw a hulking man in front of him, scuttling toward the west end of the cairn, his back to Bolan. He was carrying some kind of long gun, with its stock just visible beneath his stout right arm.

Bolan didn't consider playing by rules laid down by Hollywood and Wild West novels. He drilled a 3-round burst into the shooter's back and dropped him like a filthy habit. There was no need to examine the body as Bolan passed, or pry the weapon from beneath him. He was as dead as dirt, already leaking blood in quantities from where the rounds had ripped his flesh and vital organs, severing his spine, pulping his heart.

And now the odds were three on two.

THE FIRST SHOT stung Maksym Sushko, etching a line of fire across his left biceps without inflicting any major damage

He was quick enough to duck the second round somehow—or lucky that he stumbled—and it grazed the brim of his fedora, leaving Sushko with a thought that he had heard the wings of Death pass by him.

He was firing back then, two rounds from the pistol's magazine that was already half-depleted. When he emptied that one, if they hadn't killed him yet, he had two more in leather pouches on his belt, together with a 20-round backup he liked to carry for emergencies but had not needed yet.

Until this day.

Sushko had dropped one enemy since he'd doubled back to help Matt Cooper: one shot in the gut to pin his target, then another through the forehead while the wounded gunman screamed through an earpiece, trying to alert his leader. It had been an execution, more or less, and miles outside police guidelines, but Sushko found he didn't give a damn. If he was killed within the next few minutes, as seemed likely, he could tell whoever met him on the other side that he had done his part.

Three gunmen remained, that he was sure of, maybe more if reinforcements had been lurking in the cemetery, farther back and out of sight when Sushko left the cairn. Three was enough, but if they had not killed or wounded the American, just possibly, they had a fighting chance.

And fighting was about to start again.

He heard somebody talking to his left, another man somewhere to his right. They were not shouting back and forth, giving their game away, but rather trusting in the Bluetooth headsets to communicate. It gave them an advantage, but they should have whispered in this place where even normal tones were prone to carry like a dialogue of ghosts.

Sushko could not decide which way to go. The gunman to his right, or north, sounded a little closer than the shooter to his left. For just a second, Sushko thought of bolting westward once again, but knew the pair of them would bring him down, their automatic fire converging to annihilate him.

X would mark the bloody spot where Sushko died.

Better to face one of them, he decided—but which one? His mind was spinning, wasting precious seconds, when he heard a short, sharp burst of autofire and ducked instinctively, but heard no bullets whistling past. If they had not been aimed at him, then…

Cooper!

Sushko switched out his pistol's half-spent magazine, chose his direction, circling to the north, and went to find the tall American.

ROMAN CHERKASSKY HEARD a *zip* of automatic fire behind him, stopping in his tracks and turning just in time to see Taryk Korot go down, shot from behind. He glanced up toward the cairn's ridge with its crosses, but saw no one moving there. Another moment's hesitation, and he saw a figure start to edge around the rock pile at ground level, as if stalking him.

Cherkassky squeezed a burst out of his submachine gun, missing everything except the cairn itself, his bullets striking sparks from granite, before flying off in all directions through the boneyard. Jogging backward, trying to keep sight of his opponent, he felt loose gravel slide beneath his leather soles and fell heavily onto his backside, wasting half a dozen rounds on thin air before he released the SMG's trigger.

Stupid! Cherkassky cursed himself and scrambled to his feet, expecting to be slain at any moment, but the gunman who had killed Taryk Korot was in no rush to follow up.

Why not?

Cherkassky faced a new dilemma. Should he go back after the man he had been ordered to retrieve alive, for questioning, or focus on the bastard who had also killed one of his men? He only had two soldiers left, Bibik and Kyrylovych, both off somewhere beyond his line of sight. But he could still speak to them, through the miracle of modern technology.

"Vasyl! Nissan!" he hissed. "Come in! Where are you?"

Static answered him, some words mixed in he could not follow. Had one of the idiots damaged his headset? And where was the other? They couldn't be far off, unless...

Had they deserted him?

Cherkassky felt a surge of fury, mixed with panic, at the thought of being left alone to die. If he survived this, and the others had run out on him, he vowed to track them down and make their final hours one long, screaming litany of pain.

He tried to judge the load remaining in his weapon's magazine by hefting it, but drew a blank. He thought of switching mags but did not want to waste the time, be caught holding an empty weapon if one adversary or another suddenly sprang on him from hiding. Sweating heavily despite a chill wind rising from the distant cemetery shade, Cherkassky kept backpedaling, watching for the stalker with the automatic rifle, and glancing frequently over his shoulder to maintain the proper course to try to spot Maksym Sushko before the cop saw him.

Cherkassky thought about his cell phone, wished that he could call for reinforcements, but no one he summoned now would reach him soon enough to help. They'd only meet police arriving at the scene, and thus make matters worse.

It was his job to finish now, no matter what the cost. BOLAN ADVANCED, MOVING as cautiously as haste allowed.

He'd covered roughly half the cairn's length when he heard a scuffling of footsteps at his back and turned, crouching, to find another of the gunmen jogging toward him. This one had to have circled back from the south side on hearing gunfire, and he'd come prepared, a folding-stock Kalashnikov held at high port and ready for action.

Bolan met him with a double-tap of 3-round bursts, a chainsaw in miniature ripping the target's chest first, then his throat and jawline. The result was bloody explosions, heart and aorta ruptured and spewing, the lower face shattered beyond recognition as human. The guy tumbled backward, no sound from his lungs or his weapon until he touched down and the rifle clacked loudly on granite.

The Executioner left the body where it lay and turned back to his former course, concerned that he might have to chase his two remaining adversaries all around the cairn before he ran them down. Each minute spent on hunting brought police cars that much closer, the *bing-bong* of sirens audible already in the southern distance.

It was time to close this act and leave Bykivnia before he found himself hemmed in by troops he couldn't fight.

He heard more rapid pistol fire—Sushko?—and a short burst from a Kalashnikov, then he was off and running toward the sound, wishing the cairn and the surrounding trees had not distorted it. In seconds, Bolan reached the north end of the massive rock pile, turned the corner and found a gunner facing off against the corporal, each frozen in his shooter's stance. Behind Sushko, a crumpled figure lay supine on dusty pavement, dead eyes gaping at the slate-gray sky.

There was a short exchange between them in Ukrainian, then Bolan chimed in, shouting, "Hold it!" to distract the no-neck carrying a compact submachine gun. That intrusion brought the shooter's head around, against his better judgment, giving Sushko all the time required to shoot him three times in the chest from twelve feet out. The gunner grimaced, kept on turning toward the new arrival on the scene, and Bolan zipped him with a 3-round burst as Sushko shot him once more from the back, behind an ear.

The guy went down, shivered and died, head twisted to the right, gaze fixed at the drab gray cairn. A pond of blood spread quickly from beneath his shattered skull.

"We need to get a move on," Bolan said.

Sushko nodded and jerked a thumb over his shoulder, aiming vaguely to the south and west. "My car is there."

"Mine's out the other way," Bolan replied. "Meet you somewhere?"

"You know Rodina Mat, the Motherland statue near the Museum of the Great Patriotic War? It is impossible to miss along Ivan Mazepa Street."

"I'll find it," Bolan said. "How's thirty, forty minutes sound?"

"That should be adequate."

They parted without anything resembling a goodbye. A second meeting raised new risks, a possibility that Sushko might experience a change of heart, despite killing three men with Bolan's help. It was a chance that he would have to take.

He ran, back toward the ZAZ Vida, with an escape route plotted in advance and memorized.

10

Vozdvyzhenka, Kiev

Locals call Vozdvyzhenka "the millionaire's ghost town." Built on the ruins of a once historic neighborhood, the district's forty-two acres of lavish luxury homes were completed in 2003, with big money in mind. Ukraine's banking crisis of 2008 took the wind from its sails, with only fifty of the area's two hundred fifty homes occupied. Most days and nights, the streets were deserted, except for regular police patrols and limousines conveying residents who had endured to their expensive, widely scattered nests.

For Pavlo Voloshyn, whose only banking crisis came the time police had caught him burglarizing one, Vozdvyzhenka was perfect. Located fifteen minutes from downtown Kiev, entirely free of squatters, beggars and the other scum who made urban living a nightmare, the district was a wealthy hermit's dream come true. Security around his coral-pink, four-story mansion—the only occupied dwelling within a block—was easy to maintain. He never worried about random prowlers or solicitors, riotous parties in the structures flanking his, nothing. His men could roam the street at will in search of lurking problems, and there were no neighbors to complain.

This day, the need for tight security impressed him all the more.

The expedition to Bykivnia Graves had gone badly. Six of his men were now lying in drawers at Kiev's central morgue, reported to him by a well-paid friend with the National Police, and Voloshyn had nothing to show for the loss. He did not mourn the dead, per se. They would be easily replaced, but they had failed him and, in dying, had robbed Voloshyn of the opportunity to punish them.

It should have been a simple job. One police corporal was snooping, asking potentially damning questions, and a rumor reached Voloshyn's ears that he—this insect who aspired to heroism—was consulting with outsiders. He'd been seen with a minor functionary from the American Embassy, traipsing around Syrets'kyi Park and elsewhere like a pair of tourists, and it only took one phone call for Voloshyn to determine that the contact, a supposed deputy assistant something, was in fact an agent of the US Drug Enforcement Administration.

Voloshyn could have simply killed the corporal, but rather had him watched and followed, looking for a chance to grab his contact, sit down for a frank discussion with the meddling Westerner before he disappeared. Today was meant to be that day, but now Voloshyn's plan had crumbled into ashes and embarrassed him.

"And both of them escaped," he said, repeating it.

"Yes, sir," Mykola Shtern replied. "I'm sorry, sir."

"It's not your fault. But there must be no more mistakes."

"No, sir."

"We cannot reach inside the embassy. There's too much risk involved."

"I understand, sir."

"If it were a question of the French, perhaps, or Italy, even the Austrians, we might attempt it, but America would likely send a drone 'by accident' and ruin all of this," Voloshyn said, spreading his hands to indicate the sunken living room in which they sat, the hulking palace that surrounded it.

"Yes, sir."

"Instead, I want this damned corporal. Alive, you understand me?"

"Yes, sir."

"He will tell us everything we need to know before he feeds the Dnieper's fish."

"It will be a pleasure, sir."

"He'll be in hiding now, of course. Contact your friend, the major, and get a look inside the peasant's file. There must be something we can use to draw him out."

"Of course, sir."

The highest ranking member of the National Police staff on Pavlo Voloshyn's payroll was Major Semyon Golos, a relic from the Militsiya era who had expensive tastes and an accommodating attitude. He would accommodate Voloshyn this time, or his fat retirement fund would suddenly evaporate—along with Golos and, perhaps, his family, as well.

Hard times demanded hard choices, ruthless tactics.

And a little blood might go a long way in the end.

THE STATUE'S NAME, Rodina Mat, translated to "Mother Motherland" in English. It stood 203 feet tall and weighed 560 tons, holding aloft in its right hand a fifty-two-foot, nine-ton sword. The left hand bore a forty-three-by-twenty-six-foot shield, emblazoned with the now-defunct Soviet Union's state emblem. The looming figure rose from the rooftop of Kiev's Museum of the Great Patriotic War—otherwise known as World War II.

Corporal Sushko had been right: Bolan could not have missed the stainless-steel behemoth, glinting with sporadic highlights even underneath a gray and drizzling sky. As far as finding Sushko, that meant strolling on an open plaza near a pair of vintage battle tanks, one painted blue, the other orange, with polka dots of black and white, respectively. As Bolan passed them, he experienced the feeling of a tourist entering a strange and morbid theme park.

Sushko waited for him, sitting slumped on a retaining wall, rain beading on the brim of his fedora. He was smoking what appeared to be a miniature cigar, but from its smell could just as easily have been a stick of cinnamon.

Bolan stood over him and asked, "No tail this time, for sure?"

"No tail," Sushko confirmed.

Bolan sat beside him. His AK-12's barrel made a small *clank* beneath his raincoat, as it came to rest on the retaining wall.

"So, here's my plan," he said, "in broad strokes. Grab Voloshyn by the throat and kick his butt until he squeals. At the same time, we start working on his sometime Russian comrade."

"Bogdan Britnev."

Bolan nodded. "With some luck and perseverance, we can play them off against each other, let them do some of the heavy lifting when it comes to thinning out both sides."

"A war? In Kiev?"

Bolan nodded again. "Are you up for that?"

"I have imagined getting rid of these two and their men. It seemed to be a dream."

"We have a window," Bolan told him, "but it could go either way."

"*Da, da.* I understand."

"And if we lose, there's no plan B. No cavalry."

"You speak of crucifixion?"

Bolan had to smile at that one. "*Cava*lry, not Calvary."

"Ah, yes. Your Western cinema. John Wayne."

"He won't be joining us."

"Perhaps we shall not need him," Sushko said. "Where do we start?"

"Hitting both sides where it hurts most," Bolan replied. "I have a list of targets. You most likely know some others. Anything you've heard about that's current and important, happening over the next day or day and a half would be great."

"A drug shipment?"

"Could be. Details?"

"Voloshyn imports heroin through Belarus, originally from Afghanistan. We have an epidemic of addiction in Ukraine. Some addicts find relief with methadone, but since the occupation of Crimea, programs there have been cut off. They kill themselves in jail, buy poison on the streets, whatever. All of it good business for Voloshyn."

"And he has another shipment due?" Bolan asked.

"Coming in tonight, by lorry from Odessa."

"Tell me more."

BESARABSKY RYNOK WAS a spacious indoor market selling every possible variety of meat, fruit, vegetable and flower found in or imported to Ukraine. Major Semyon Golos, no gourmet and certainly no chef, still felt at home there, browsing among others like himself who could afford the prices without haggling for a discount—which, in any case, would not have been forthcoming. He enjoyed the sights and smells, even the gutted rabbits with their skins on, paws pinned back to show the gleaming insides.

Golos enjoyed it all, but this was not a normal shopping trip. The summons he'd received had killed his appetite. Despite his rank, his prominence within Ukraine's National Police, Major Golos could not ignore his master's voice. The unrecorded, untaxed salary Golos received from Pavlo Voloshyn far exceeded his official monthly pay. At that rate, some corruption was anticipated, but Golos had sold his soul to Voloshyn's branch of the Ukrainian mafia, and there could be no turning back short of ruin or suicide.

Neither of which held any appeal for the major.

He found the sidewalk café he was seeking and sat by himself at a table near the curb. That might have been a risky proposition if he were in uniform, but he wore a conservative business suit instead, and his face was not well known outside headquarters. When the boxy black ZIL-4112R limousine pulled up and sat there, idling, Golos left his untouched glass of vodka behind and climbed into the car through a back door that opened like magic.

Pavlo Voloshyn sat alone in the backseat, leaving Golos to take a jump seat facing him, so that they were not riding side by side. Before the limo pulled out into traffic, making smaller cars slow down and wait, the mobster said, "One of your officers is after me."

"Is he?" It was a foolish thing to say, Golos immediately realized, but he could not take it back.

"And working with a foreigner, from what I'm told."

"By whom, if I may ask?" Golos queried.

"Another foreigner. Intelligence. That's all you need to know."

"It helps to know if he or she has proved reliable," the major said.

"Extremely so."

"In that case, I assure you that whatever has been done occurred without my knowledge or approval."

"That is what worries me, Semyon. It means that someone higher up has bypassed you, or that you've lost control of your subordinates. In either case, it bodes ill for our future as a team."

"You have my word that—"

"What I have," Voloshyn interrupted him, "is a small window within which to find your man and learn exactly who he is collaborating with. After the recent setbacks in New York, I fear it may be an American. Their DEA perhaps, or FBI, even the ATF pursuing weapons."

Golos knew certain details of the trouble in New York— not only ruination for the mafia's various enterprises but considerable loss of life. A kind of massacre, in fact.

"And do you know the officer involved?" he asked.

"A lowly corporal on the force, for God's sake. No one in the scheme of things. His name is Maksym Sushko."

"While I've never personally heard of him," Golos replied, "it should be simple to locate him."

"I hope so," Voloshyn said, "for your sake."

"There is no need to be threatening," Golos stated stiffly.

"When I threaten you, you'll know it. You most likely will be bleeding and near death. This is a warning, one friend to another. Pull your man in, question him and find out who he's working for. It clearly is not you."

"And when I have that information?"

"Tell me where and how to find the foreigner, then make your faithless corporal disappear."

"It might be wiser—"

"Simply do as you are told!" Voloshyn snapped. "*I* am not paying *you* to question *me*."

"No, sir. I mean, yes, sir. Of course, sir."

"Take us back to the café," Voloshyn told his driver.

The major's mind was spinning, trying hard to process what Voloshyn had revealed to him. He'd questioned whether it was true initially, but that would make no difference now. He had a name, a rank and orders from his secret master to perform a certain task.

Voloshyn had already signed Corporal Sushko's death sentence with his order.

Now Golos was required to carry out the execution, after he obtained whatever information his subordinate possessed.

And if the corporal died professing innocence, regardless of the means employed, what then? Golos could go back to Voloshyn and admit his failure—or he could concoct a fable from thin air to make himself appear proficient at his job. But when that lie led nowhere in the end…

Then it would be *his* end, once and for all.

Religion had been actively suppressed when Ukraine was controlled from Moscow, between 1917 and 1991, but Golos had been born to closet Eastern Orthodox believers, secretly instructed in the church's rituals while public school drilled him on atheism. The result, after the USSR had collapsed, was that Golos knew all the terms and rites of his supposed religion, but he had no faith.

Until today.

Now, he was wondering if he should pray that Corporal Sushko knew a name to give him, which he would in turn pass on to Pavlo Voloshyn. Only in that way could he save himself—and by eliminating Sushko once he was milked dry of information on the foreigner.

Salvation via murder?

Well, it wouldn't be the first time in this world, or in his personal experience.

Major Golos knew where a great number of bodies had been buried. He had planted some of them himself, and ordered other graves to be prepared. If that did not seem like a policeman's work, it was a dose of hard reality on life within Ukraine.

The limo stopped, and when the door did not open spontaneously, Golos reached out for the latch and exited, nearly—but not quite—stumbling on the café's curb. He turned to shut the heavy door and heard Voloshyn say, "Twelve hours. That's your limit, Semyon."

Face slack, cursing silently, he watched the ZIL-4112R glide away and disappear.

Fishing inside a pocket of his overcoat, Golos retrieved his cell phone and punched the speed-dial number for his office. When his aide-de-camp responded midway through the second ring, Golos did not identify himself. The young man knew his voice and recognized his mood.

"I'm coming back from lunch," he said. "Have Sergeant Holovatsky waiting for me when I get there."

"Yes, sir!"

Golos killed the link and pocketed the phone. He had not brought a vehicle and driver to his meeting with Voloshyn, fearing a police squad car might be recognized. Instead, he walked two blocks to catch a trolleybus.

Sergeant Vanko Holovatsky was a pit bull cast in human form. Once given an assignment he would not relent, and unlike certain other police officers, it did not matter to him whether he was hunting common criminals, subversives or one of his own. A job was simply that, and if it brought some small reward when he was done, so much the better.

Holovatsky also had a knack for squeezing information out of a reluctant suspect. The Americans had once described it as "enhanced interrogation," fond as ever of their euphemisms. Other nations, other law-enforcement agencies, used different terms—and sometimes squabbled over whether the results could be relied upon.

In this case, Major Golos was willing to take what he could get, as soon as possible.

There was no viable alternative.

11

Kiev Oblast, Ukraine

Mack Bolan peered through the Steiner 5-25x scope on his KNT-308 rifle, watching an old cabin cruiser nose in toward the western shore of the Dnieper River, seven hundred yards in front of him. Maksym Sushko lay beside him in a grove of trees, watching the craft through small binoculars, counting the men who had arrived to meet it in a VEPR multipurpose off-road vehicle.

"Four guns," he said.

"No problem," Bolan answered.

They were roughly halfway between Kiev on the south, and cursed Chernobyl to the north. No one lived full-time in this gray zone between Ukraine's capital and the ghost town blighted by a nuclear reactor accident in April 1986, still the subject of ghastly rumors and low-budget horror films thirty years later. The drug runners had chosen their location wisely, and it worked as well for Bolan in his role of Executioner.

"You let them land the cargo?" Sushko asked, confirming it.

"Just like we planned. The boat won't want to stick around. Its crew is finished when they put the load ashore."

It was easier that way for Bolan, too. The bolt-action KNT-308 held five rounds of 7.62 mm ammunition in a 5-round detachable box magazine, replaceable within seconds. Its effective range was rated at one thousand meters with the 122-grain full-metal-jacket rounds he loaded, hurling them downrange at 2,396 feet per second, striking their target with 1,555 foot-pounds of energy. More than enough to do the job.

"This still feels strange," Sushko said. "In the past, I have always attempted to arrest— What do you call them? Subjects?"

"Targets," Bolan said, correcting him.

"Yes," the Ukrainian policeman agreed. "But just to kill them…"

"Take my word for it. They'd do the same to you without a second thought."

"Of course, but…"

"We've been over this. If you're changing your mind, crawl back and wait for me at the car. I'll drop you off when we get back to—"

"No! I'm with you. I'm simply getting used to it."

"Well, now's the time."

The boat had grounded, unloading had begun and, as Bolan had calculated from experience, the men who'd made delivery weren't wasting any time. They might be Belarusians, but they'd know the penalties applied for running heroin by judges in Ukraine: up to twelve years in prison for holding 250 grams or more of heroin.

The packages coming ashore down there were kilo lots, and Bolan counted twenty of them passed from hand to hand before the boat crew pushed off from the riverbank and turned northward, for home.

When shooting started, they would not return to join in the festivities.

"HURRY. WE NEED to move," Theo Waksman said, watching while his three companions finished shifting packages of heroin into the VEPR SUV.

"We're hurrying," Olexandro Horbulin replied, "while you stand there and watch."

Waksman brandished his stubby AG-043 assault weapon. "I *am* watching," he answered back. "And you'll be damned glad of it if there's trouble."

"Trouble?" When he spoke, Eugen Kuznets put on a mocking tone. "When in the past two years have we had any trouble here?"

"One time is one too many," Waksman countered, and repeated, "Hurry up!"

They still had some two dozen packages to pick up from the riverbank and transfer to their vehicle. One hundred kilos was a big load, although smaller than some riverboats delivered to the docks of the Pecherskyi District in downtown Kiev, disguised in cases of machine parts, farming tools or Eastern artwork. Those could run into a thousand kilos, sometimes double, even triple that, feeding the habits of Ukraine's addicts, spreading the plague of HIV faster than any other European nation with their shared needles. Junkies aside, Ukraine was recognized as an important transit country for the flow of heroin during the thirteen years since the American invasion of Afghanistan.

Waksman could have laid down his rifle and pitched in, but he was lazy. That was one reason he had become a gangster, coupled with his love of easy money and the atavistic thrill he always got from violence.

Yakiv Kovel had almost reached the jet-black SUV with two more packages when his head exploded like a ripe melon with a firework packed inside, except that it was nearly silent, just a *pop* and crimson *splash* without the ringing *bang*. Kovel stopped dead in his tracks, the blood and gray matter cascading down his torso, then he dropped and fell face forward on the oilskin packages he carried.

Only then did Waksman hear the echo of a rifle shot.

"Snayper!" he shouted to the others, even as he dived for cover in the VEPR's shadow, hoping that its bulk would spare him from incoming fire.

The sharp reverberation of a second shot rolled past him, toward the river, and he saw one of the Belarusians staring back at him, already something like a quarter mile up range. The sniper wasn't taking shots at *them*, of course, because they had nothing he cared a damn about.

It was the heroin, obviously. Whoever killed Kovel wanted it, and Waksman knew his life was forfeit if he went back to Pavlo Voloshyn empty-handed. Guarding the heroin was his job, and if it cost him his life, at least he would not die a traitor to his chosen Family.

Waksman popped up to fire a short burst from his AG-043, uphill and in the general direction that he thought the shots had come from. He hit nothing, as expected, but at least he made some noise.

BOLAN HAD WATCHED the first thug drop without emotion, long ago inured to sudden death up close and personal, reflected in a sniper's scope or at arm's length in mortal combat. By the time the headless man went down he was already tracking, swinging toward his second target of the four men sent to claim the heroin and drive it to Kiev.

The other three were quick; he gave them that. Their leader shouted something Bolan couldn't understand, barely a whisper at the distance he was firing from, then pitched himself headlong behind their SUV. The remaining men were slower, at least marginally. One of them, encumbered by his own armload of oilskin parcels, had been walking several yards behind the first man Bolan shot and had to blink his eyes clear from the scarlet mist painting his startled face. The other had been placing his load in the SUV and simply dived inside the vehicle, yanking the double back doors shut behind him as he dropped from sight.

That was a problem, more so if he had the VEPR's key, but Bolan kept his wits about him, doing one job at a time. His second target was the only man still visible, that one dropping his packages and turning toward the vehicle, right hand outstretched to grab the passenger-door handle, likely praying speed would help him get safely inside.

But in the real world, not so much.

The next round out of Bolan's KNT was lower than the first. It drilled the drug runner's chest from left to right, the FMJ slug burrowing through lungs and heart and all, erupting from his right armpit below his upraised arm. There was no question of surviving the hit.

That left two, and one of them—the guy behind the VEPR's broad front end—sprang up to fire a burst of autofire in Bolan's general direction, just as a reminder he was still alive. The slugs came nowhere close to Bolan or to Sushko, hardly aimed, but made a rattling, rippling sound over their heads.

The shooter dropped back out of sight before Bolan could tag him, leaving Bolan to devise a better plan.

MAKSYM SUSHKO LAY deathly still and watched the mobsters dying through his binoculars. He'd plugged his ears with cotton, on advice from the American, before Cooper fired his first rifle shot. The result had been dramatic, even horrifying.

He had grown accustomed to brutality, investigating urban crimes for the National Police, but he had never seen a man's head detonate before, as if someone had stuffed a hand grenade into his mouth. The body lingered upright for a heartbeat, maybe two, blood pumping from the stub of neck, then dropped as if the dead man were a puppet and someone had slashed his strings. The second gangster's death was immediate.

Two of the smugglers still survived, but Sushko could not see them, one hiding behind the SUV, the other man somewhere inside it now. Even if he *could* see them, neither his Bandayevsky RB-12 shotgun, with its twenty-inch barrel, nor his standard-issue Makarov PM sidearm would reach the enemy in front of him, at Cooper's chosen range.

The truth be told, Sushko was satisfied to watch for now, and even that had made him slightly queasy, disregarding his abilities as an experienced policeman.

Beside him, the American lined up another shot, though neither of the two surviving drug runners were immediately visible. His next round smashed one of the windows in the SUVs double back doors, pebbling the safety glass and blowing it away. There was no hope of that shot striking anyone, but when he fired the next round, Cooper was aiming lower, landing number four where it would pierce the SUV's fuel tank and start a dribble flowing there.

The low octane of diesel fuel prevented its explosion from igniting the VEPR, but at least the shot would keep the smuggling rig from going much of anywhere if its survivors managed to escape. Cooper's last round took out the right-rear tire, air hissing from it as it settled on its chrome rim in the dust.

He was reloading when Sushko inquired, "Now what?"

"Now we hang on a little while and see what happens next."

THEO WAKSMAN STILL had no idea exactly where the rifle shots were coming from, but it was clear the sniper knew what he was doing, and the lonely setting offered no pros-

pect for rescue in the near future. The men who had delivered Pavlo Voloshyn's illicit cargo would not send him
any help, for fear of being linked to the attack and all that
would be revealed because of it. Nor would a stray police
patrol pass by in time to save Waksman—and if it did, his
destination would be one of Ukraine's 131 penitentiaries,
condemned by various human rights organizations for torture and other harsh treatment of inmates.

No. On balance, he would rather take his chances with
the sniper and a sudden death than twenty years at Zam-
kova Correctional Colony or one of its equivalents.

What could he do?

Reaching his adversary seemed impossible. Waksman
could tell that several hundred yards of open ground lay
between them, meaning that he could not reach the gunman without being cut down in his tracks. Likewise, he
could not rise and take the time to aim a killing burst from
his assault rifle, lest he go down like Kovel and Horbulin.
Eugen Kuznets was hiding in the SUV, immobilized, but
Waksman had the vehicle's ignition key and—

The idea struck him, pristine in its simplicity. If he could
reach the driver's door alive and duck into the vehicle, stay
low and shielded by its bodywork until he got the engine
running, he could simply drive away!

All right. He knew the SUV had taken hits, could smell
the leaking diesel fuel and felt it listing where one of its
tires was flattened, but so what? The VEPR was designed
originally as a military vehicle for rough terrain, nicknamed
the "wild boar" for its ruggedness. If Waksman could not
make it all the way back to Kiev, at least he could drive
partway and escape the sniper who was bent on killing him.

As to the heroin, well, part of it was loaded now. The
rest could go to hell. If Waksman tried to save it now, he
would be dead and his boss would have nothing.

By the gods, Voloshyn should regard him as a hero if he pulled it off!

The driver's seat was on the VEPR's left and fairly close to where Waksman was huddled, staying low and out of sight. Putting his plan into action, he crept around the black SUV's bumper, past the left-front tire, grateful the SUV was jacked up nineteen inches off the ground and granting extra cover from his enemy.

Unless the enemy had moved while he was working out his getaway.

Expecting to be shot at any second, Waksman reached the driver's door, rose slowly to his knees and opened it. The surge inside required a Herculean effort, after crouching on the ground so long, but Waksman managed it. A second later, he was slumped in the driver's seat, twisting the key, while Kuznets yammered questions at him from the storage bay in back.

"Shut up!" he snapped and put the rolling monster into gear, released its parking brake and stood on the accelerator.

BOLAN HAD ONE chance to stop the SUV's retreat, and only one. Disabling the engine with a long shot through the hood was problematic, and the VEPR still had fuel enough to run for miles back toward Kiev, or northward to Chernobyl if the driver lost his bearings and escaped that way. Hitting the man himself should do it, but the off-road vehicle's tinted windows meant he would be nearly shooting blind.

One helpful thing was, once Bolan's human target got the VEPR rolling, he immediately swung it toward the highway half a mile back from the river, angling toward the asphalt. Thinking quickly, Bolan tried to put himself inside the fleeing mobster's mind.

Would he be sitting upright in the driver's seat, risking a window shot? Highly unlikely. Low profile was the way to go, peeking from time to time over the SUV's dashboard to keep himself on track.

And that meant firing through the driver's door, assuming that the VEPR wasn't armored in the military style for runs like this, retrieving heroin worth millions for the mob boss of Kiev.

Taking the gamble, Bolan pegged the Steiner telescopic sight's G2B Mil-Dot illuminated reticle on the SUV driver's door, holding the four-post crosshair configuration about where a tall man's hips and waist should be. He fired once, smoothly worked the bolt and put two more FMJ rounds directly through the door, hoping at least one of the slugs would drill the driver where he sat and scramble his insides.

It took another moment, but at last the VEPR seemed to lose direction, swinging back toward where it had come from, in a wide loop toward the Dnieper River. Bolan watched it through his scope, the driver dead or helpless as the SUV charged downslope, approached the water's edge, then plunged into the river. It drifted with the current for a moment, slowly sinking out of sight, then disappeared without a trace.

"All gone!" Sushko exhaled.

"Not all," Bolan corrected him. "They left at least a quarter of the load on shore."

"What shall we do with it?"

Rising, Bolan slung the sniper rifle over his left shoulder, then stooped to retrieve the AK-12. "I'll shoot the hell out of it," he replied, "and leave it to the elements."

"There will be happy birds," his sidekick said, grinning.

"But not back in Kiev," Bolan replied. "While I'm doing that, I need you to make two phone calls."

12

Vozdvyzhenka, Kiev

Pavlo Voloshyn lived a short distance from the center of the capital, a brief walk from the massive Dreamtown shopping mall replete with high-end retail shops, food market, cinema and other entertainments. Not that he ever actually *walked* around the city, mind you. Not when he had men to drive him and so many rivals of his Family were waiting for a chance to kill him.

Such was life, and the old saying had proved accurate: it *was* lonely at the top, in spite of the rewards.

He thought about the heroin whose street value was roughly two hundred million US dollars. Theo Waksman should have called by now, but Voloshyn knew things happened on a drug run, whether the delivery was late or they had trouble on the highway. Waksman had not let him down before, and there was no reason to think...

His burner phone buzzed and the mobster answered before it could sound a second time. "Talk to me," he ordered.

"But what should I tell you?" asked a voice he did not recognize. "Should I pretend your heroin is safe and sound?

It's not. Should I say your four soldiers are alive and well, when they are dead?"

"Who is this?" Voloshyn demanded.

"Your worst nightmare," the caller replied. "We have never met, but that time is approaching, Pavlo Voloshyn."

Through clenched teeth, he replied, "You know my name. What's yours?"

"That's not important. What you *should* be asking is who hired me to destroy your shipment and advise you of the fact."

"Well? Tell me, then. I'm waiting."

"Your old friend, Bogdan Britnev," the caller answered, almost gloating. "It would seem that your alliance is dissolved."

"*You* say."

"And you have no reason to trust me, naturally. Why even believe your shipment and your men are lost, until you check for yourself. By all means, be my guest. Waste more time, when your hours are running out."

The line went dead. Voloshyn realized he held the burner in a death grip, knuckles blanched, arm trembling, and he made a conscious effort to relax.

His next call went to Theo Waksman's burner phone, but it went to voice mail after six unanswered rings. Staring from his picture window toward the Dnieper River, Voloshyn tried to wrap his mind around what he'd been told and what, if true, it meant for him, his Family and for their future.

First, assume the worst: What if the heroin was lost? Voloshyn barely thought about his men, compared to what he'd paid the dealer in Belarus for one hundred kilos of prime heroin from Afghanistan, refined to pharmaceutical purity that would have let him cut it for the street at least six times. That tab was twenty million US dollars, and he *did* know that amount in native currency by heart: 421 million *hryvnia* straight out of his pocket and thrown to the winds like a ton of confetti.

But no—worse yet, it had been *stolen* from him by an enemy. And if he dared to trust the nameless caller—who, in fact, might be deceiving him for reasons Voloshyn could not presently divine—that enemy had duped him, posing as an ally as they went about their business, acting as if they were partners.

Bogdan Britnev.

They were not friends, of course, and Voloshyn trusted Britnev no more than he placed faith in any other man, but they had operated for some years now with an understanding, with no violation of that deal on either side. Why would Britnev suddenly decide to kill four of Voloshyn's men and steal one hundred kilos of heroin that had just arrived from Belarus?

Why did the man do anything? For money.

Next question: If true, who had betrayed Britnev to Voloshyn?

He would think about that next, while he prepared himself for war.

Svyatoshyn-Nyvkiy, Kiev

Bogdan Britnev glanced at his cell phone's LED window and did not recognize the number of the call that had distracted him from paperwork: one thousand AK-105 assault rifles inbound from Russia, destined for the Right Front in its preparation for a possible invasion from the north and east. He thought about ignoring it, letting the call go to voice mail, then picked it up instead.

"Hello," he said.

A male voice unfamiliar to him, speaking in Ukrainian, demanded, "Why did you steal Pavlo's heroin?"

After a blink of stunned surprise, Britnev shot back, "What are you babbling about? Who *is* this?"

"Never mind," the male voice answered, almost whispering. "He knows!"

Blustering, Britnev said, "I don't know if you have the wrong phone number or if you're insane, but—"

"*You* must be insane, Bogdan, to think that you could rob Voloshyn, kill four of his men and—"

Cutting through the stranger's accusations, heedless of the sudden ringing in his ears, Britnev insisted, "You have reached the wrong number. Try again and get the right party next time!"

He cut the link, hand trembling as he switched off his cell phone, avoiding any callback from the madman.

Then he had to ask himself: What if the caller was not mad?

Oh, he was *wrong*, of course. Britnev had stolen no drugs from Pavlo Voloshyn, much less murdered any of his soldiers. But if *someone* had, and Pavlo thought *he* was that foolish someone…

Britnev slumped back in his desk chair, paperwork and AK-105s forgotten. If Pavlo suspected him of such betrayal, it could only mean a shooting war. He needed to get ahead of that, find out exactly what—if anything—had happened, and if there was murder in the wind, convince Pavlo somehow that he was not to blame for any losses suffered by the Voloshyn Family.

He switched on the cell phone once more, speed-dialed Voloshyn's private number, cleared his throat and spoke decisively when one of Pavlo's housemen answered. "Bogdan Britnev, calling Mr. Voloshyn."

"Hang on a minute."

Britnev hung on as ordered. Seconds later, Voloshyn's voice came on the line, raging. "You traitorous prick! To pull this shit on me, of all people! You've signed your own death warrant! Count the hours until I—"

Britnev ended the call, emotions seething in his chest, thoughts swirling in his brain. He was fearful and furious at the same time, outraged by the false accusation, shocked by the prospect of an all-out war with Pavlo's brutal Family.

The theft and murders obviously *had* occurred, and he was being framed for them. By whom? That stymied Britnev. He could think of no one in Ukraine who would attack Voloshyn in that manner, much less blame *him* for the raid. It had to be a devious conspiracy, and while Britnev could name a hundred men who hated him enough to do it, none possessed the power, skill or finesse to pull it off.

A mystery. He hated that in fiction, all the more so in real life, when it affected him.

And this one, if he could not sort it out damned quickly, just might get him killed.

Voloshyn was already on the warpath, by the sound of it. He would not speak to Britnev beyond shouting accusations and obscenities. Unless they were to fight—and that meant to the death—Britnev would have to find a mediator whom Pavlo would listen to, respect and trust.

Did such a man exist?

Before he puzzled over that, another mystery, Britnev had one more call to make. He needed reinforcements against Pavlo and, off-hand, could only think of one man who might help.

"HE HUNG UP on me," Maksym Sushko said, sounding surprised.

Bolan smiled at him from the driver's seat as they headed

southbound, and said, "I'm not surprised. You gave it to him pretty good."

"You said 'sound angry.'"

"And you nailed it. He'll be thinking now, just like Voloshyn."

"They will go to war?" The corporal sounded nervous now.

"That was the plan. We'll have to watch and stir things up a bit more, making sure."

"I'm thinking of the decent people in Kiev."

"We talked about the risks," Bolan reminded him. "You still signed on."

"Yes, yes, I know. But if they choose some crowded place to fight…"

"Not likely. It would go against the grain for both of them."

"But seeking a surprise, an ambush…"

"Both are on their guard now. You just saw to that."

"And where will we be?" Sushko asked him.

"In the middle of it. I still want to stir the pot a little. Shake some cages."

"Keeping up the pressure?"

"That's the ticket. Something that will keep Voloshyn holed up in his house while the other side gets agitated and goes looking for him."

"Ah." Sushko was getting it. "A safer battleground?"

"Best we can do, inside Kiev."

"But the few residents remaining still have influence, Voloshyn maybe most of all. He's bound to call for the police if he's attacked."

"Too late, with any luck at all," Bolan replied.

"You trust them to behave a certain way," Sushko observed.

"With room for deviations. Psychopaths like these two

have no conscience as we know it, no regard for others but as tools to gain whatever they desire. They weigh responses to a threat by what it costs, the risks involved for *them*. In this case, Voloshyn and Britnev both should see eliminating his primary rival as the pathway to relief. I want to keep them thinking that way and direct the action toward Voloshyn's home base if I can."

"And how will you—will *we*—do that?"

"Make Britnev think Voloshyn's making moves against him, while Voloshyn feels he's safest staying in Vozd-vyzhenka."

"More raids," Sushko said, cutting to the chase.

"More raids," Bolan agreed. "For Britnev, one or two hits ought to do it. And ideally, for Voloshyn, we'd take out his nearest likely hideaway."

"I know where that is," Sushko said. "A house in Obolon, between the river and Verbova Street."

"And for Britnev?" Bolan asked.

"There are several. He deals primarily in weapons, but is also fond of human trafficking to Eastern Europe and beyond. He has what you might call a stable for his women near the Kontraktova Square in the Podil. And there is a warehouse for the guns beside the river, in the Holosi-ivskyi District."

"That should do it, if we pull them off."

"All three?" Sushko seemed startled. "Do we have the time?"

"We'll make time," Bolan said. "No sleeping on this tour of duty, soldier. Steer me toward Voloshyn's home away from home."

Podilskyi District, Kiev

LOCATED ON THE Dnieper River near the modern city center Podil was Kiev's oldest residential neighborhood, know for its lovely pre-Soviet architecture, quiet streets and a wide selection of restaurants. It hosted one of the city's oldest, most prestigious schools—the National University of Kyiv Mohylanskaya Academy—plus numerous art galleries and the capital's only funicular railway.

None of which meant anything to Samuil Skorokhod on that afternoon.

Normally, he took pride in Kiev's past and its historic sites, as in the many others found throughout Ukraine. He was a nationalist first and foremost, to the point that some within his homeland—even more outside it—called him an agitator, rabble-rouser, terrorist, et cetera. As leader of the armed and militant Right Front, Skorokhod would plead guilty to those charges any day and wear them as a badge of pride while battling Russian intervention in Ukraine.

This day, though, he was more concerned with just staying alive, and what that might cost him.

Bogdan Britnev had spoken to him briefly on the phone, but there was no confusion about what he was demanding. On a moment's notice, he required Skorokhod and the Right Front to defend him from Pavlo Voloshyn's syndicate, falsely accused—or so he said—of waging unprovoked attacks against the city's top crime Family.

Skorokhod was now in the bizarre position of fielding his paramilitary troops to guard a Russian criminal against Ukrainian mobsters, the lot of whom he equally despised and would have gladly slaughtered if it were within his power. Sadly, if he killed Britnev or let Voloshyn kill him, that wiped out the Right Front's leading source of arms and ammunition for their battle to protect Ukraine's people and their integrity as a nation.

His bargain with Bogdan Britnev was Faustian but still a fact of life. Thus far, aside from making Samuil Skorokhod bitterly chastise himself in private moments, it had worked out well enough, but now the devil called upon him for a favor he could not refuse, even if it destroyed him and the righteous movement he had built from the ground up.

What would his men say if he took the time to brief them on his labyrinthine problem? Would they storm out, turn their guns upon him in a rage or recognize that politics demanded unpleasant compromises every day? Their movement's "purity" was based on his collaboration with an ancient enemy who might well turn against them if and when Russia launched an invasion of Ukraine.

One thing was certain about Britnev: given any choice, he always sided with a winner, and Russia's military—ranked fifth largest in the world, with 771,000 active duty personnel, estimates of its reservists ranging between two and twenty million—had Ukraine's 250,000, with another 700,000 in reserve, as good as beaten in advance.

His country's last stand might be glorious, but as to victory, unless the world at large weighed in somehow against Moscow, it was a hopelessly lost cause.

Which Samuil Skorokhod would die for, if it came to that.

But first, he had to risk his life and all his soldiers on behalf of Bogdan Britnev.

13

Obolonskyi District, Kiev

Pavlo Voloshyn's hideout wasn't spectacular—at least, not from the outside—but it was on a cul-de-sac and easily defensible if the Ukrainian Mob boss called out his troops in force. While troops were probably receiving urgent calls to rally round their boss, they hadn't flocked to Obolon as yet. Bolan and Sushko had an open window to attack the house, and they weren't wasting any time.

Bolan had brought his AK-12 assault rifle, his Glock 18 for backup, plus his RPG with two incendiary rockets and some F1 fragmentation grenades. Sushko had his Bandayevsky RB-12 shotgun and Makarov PM sidearm as they approached Voloshyn's second home, scaled its back wall and made a beeline for the patio's glass sliding door.

The door was locked, so Bolan shattered it with a short burst from his Kalashnikov and went inside, with Sushko on his heels. Two of Voloshyn's soldiers were in residence, a cushy job in peacetime as they lounged around and watched the godfather's TV, eating his food and drinking his beer. They both responded to the crash of gunfire from what Bolan saw was the rec room, stocked with games on par with what you'd find in any upscale video arcade. One man turned up shirtless, likely caught while working out in Voloshyn's gym; the other one was dressed but had his tie askew, clearly surprised to find himself confronting well-armed, uninvited company.

The rec room specialized in make-believe shooting, but the mobster's men were packing real-life SR-2 Veresk machine pistols, chambered for 9 mm blunt-nosed viper rounds.

Bolan dropped one of them, with a 3-round burst from his AK that slammed the dead man back against the door frame where he'd entered seconds earlier. Sushko took down the other gunner with a buckshot charge that gutted him and left him writhing for a moment on the white shag carpeting, red now, before he shivered out and died.

They swept the house for stragglers, cleaners, cooks, whatever, and found no one else in residence. Leaving the way they'd come, Bolan paused long enough to load his RPG with a 105 mm TBG-7V thermobaric round weighing ten pounds, firing it through the rec room's open doorway to the patio and watching it explode inside. A ball of fire consumed the games, corpses and all that was at ground zero, then spread swiftly through Pavlo Voloshyn's house. By the time Bolan had followed Sushko back over the wall, the place was totally engulfed, staining the blue suburban sky with smoke.

If Pavlo Voloshyn had fled his first home in the millionaire's graveyard, he'd need some other place to run and hide.

Vozdvyzhenka, Kiev

VOLOSHYN GOT THE news from one of his police contacts and thought he took it fairly well, under the circumstances

Members of the city's fire department arrived too late to save his home in Obolon and were impeded by the nature of the fire's accelerant, a thermobaric chemical often referred to as a fuel-air explosive that included two separate charges: one to detonate the bomb—in this case, he was told, a rocket-propelled grenade—while the other mixed with atmospheric oxygen and caused a massive blast wave.

It was a total loss, Voloshyn was told, and he was lucky from a legal standpoint that the fire had been contained before it spread to other homes around the cul-de-sac.

His head was pounding, driving Voloshyn to use one of his Imitrex inhalers for the budding migraine, washing down its sour aftertaste with Ukrainka Platinum vodka. After the third shot, he began to think his skull would not explode and he could focus on the problem of survival.

After summoning his soldiers, every last man of his army, he called Major Semyon Golos on his private line and waited for the officer to pick up on the fourth shrill ring. "You know who this is?" he demanded, after Golos said "Hello."

"I do."

"Have you been told about the fire?"

"What fire?" the major asked, all innocence.

Barely holding back a litany of obscenities, the mobster shifted gears. "How goes the search for you-know-who?"

"I ordered his superior to contact him, with no success," Golos said. "Now there's an active search ongoing for the lost corporal, but so far he hasn't been located. He is not at home. His few kinfolk profess that they've not seen or heard from him."

"He simply disappeared?"

"It would appear so, for the moment, but—"

"Has it occurred to you that I'm under attack? For all I

know, this officer of yours and his foreign friend are part of it."

"I seriously doubt that Corporal—"

"No names on the telephone!"

"Of course. I seriously doubt that he would be involved in something of this kind. As to the foreigner, we have no idea who he is or where to find him."

"What good are you, then?" Voloshyn demanded.

"I—"

"Take money every month and give me…what? A helpless shrug? Excuses?"

"I am trying," Golos answered weakly. "We shall find the missing officer, I promise you."

"Perhaps too late to help me. In the meantime, I have information that an ally has decided to betray me."

"Who?" the major asked.

"A certain Russian of our mutual acquaintance."

"You don't mean it!"

"No, of course not," the mobster said with a sneer. "I only called to play a joke on you."

"A joke?"

"Of course I mean it!" Voloshyn raged. "Now what do you plan to do about it?"

"Well, I…"

"Plan your answer carefully," Voloshyn said, warning him. "Your very life depends on it."

"As soon as we are off the line, I'm mobilizing every officer at my disposal. If required, I can contact the commanding general of the Ukraine National Guard."

"And how would you explain it to the National Guard?" the mobster challenged.

"I'll make something up!"

"No. Forget that. Make do with your officers, but be

damned sure that we can trust them. No more meddlers like your corporal."

"I guarantee it," Golos said.

"And I expect that guarantee to be fulfilled," Voloshyn snapped. "Failure on your part will be fatal, I assure you."

Holosiivskyi District, Kiev

THE HOLOSIIVSKYI DISTRICT was relatively new, fabricated by the Kiev City Council in September of 2001, described by its online promotions as "abounding in stimulating energy and tourist sites." One of the latter was the 140-acre Holosiivskyi National Park, including, among other things, pristine forest, miles of trails for sightseeing on foot or via bicycle, playgrounds, campgrounds, carnival rides, paddle boats, cafés and a hotel.

The crowds had thinned by waning afternoon, when Bolan and Maksym Sushko approached the warehouse labeled Zeleni Zrostannya Promyslovosti, which Sushko translated to read "Green Growth Industries." As far as he could say, the only green growth underway was money banked by Bogdan Britnev from the sale of outlawed weapons to whoever had the ready cash on hand.

If Bolan had his way, the Russian was about to have a going-out-of-business sale.

They checked around the place, making their presence obvious to anyone who might be lurking on the grounds, but found no sign of any watchmen standing guard over the property. That lapse surprised the Executioner, but Sushko told him Britnev's reputation generally kept sane thieves at bay, while any criminals, extremist paramilitary groups and such had sense enough to deal with Britnev honestly, secure in understanding that he never ratted on them to police and sold his wares to all sides equally, without discrimination.

When they were satisfied the warehouse was unoccupied, Bolan shot off the dead bolt on a door in back and took his RPG-7 inside, while Sushko stood watch on the loading dock. The place wasn't exactly cavernous, like some industrial warehouses, but it was about two hundred feet from end to end, with wooden crates piled up to six feet high in rows, with aisles between them wide enough for a forklift to navigate.

A decent shooting gallery.

Two of the three rounds Bolan carried with him were the standard PG-7VL HEAT variety—short for high-explosive anti-tank warheads—weighing 4.85 pounds apiece. He fired them both downrange, one toward the farthest row of crates off to his left, skipping two rows before he loosed the second one, ears ringing as he backed out of the warehouse with the final rocket dangling from his hand.

Outside, he loaded his launcher with the thermobaric round and sent it smoking through the back door that he'd exited, no great precision aiming to it, knowing that wherever it exploded it would gut the warehouse with a firestorm, fusing metal, setting off the stores of ammunition, maybe even some explosives if Britnev kept them in stock. Before the flames gushed back at him, across the loading dock, Bolan and Sushko were already back inside the ZAZ Vida, rolling away from there and on toward their third Kiev target of the afternoon.

"You make a lot of enemies," the corporal said. "Is it like this, no matter where you go?"

"Not always," Bolan said, "but mostly yes. The good news is, my enemies don't have to stew about it very long."

"Stew?" Sushko frowned across at him. "That is a recipe, I think, with meat and vegetables?"

"The other kind," Bolan corrected him. "Meaning to fret or worry."

"Ah. So not the same. That is *tushkovane m'yaso*."

"Whatever," Bolan said. "I try to put them all out of my misery."

"We may not have the luxury of using the grenade launcher at our next stop," Sushko suggested.

"Fair enough," Bolan replied. "As long as Britnev gets the message."

Svyatoshyn-Nyvkiy, Kiev

BOGDAN BRITNEV RECEIVED the message loud and clear. He simply didn't know where it was coming from. After the call from the person he took to be a spokesman for Pavlo Voloshyn, he was focused on Kiev's crime Family to the exclusion of all else. Britnev had no idea why Voloshyn or anyone associated with him should suspect him, Britnev, of hijacking heroin and murdering the couriers, but he was clearly being blamed for that offense and targeted for grim reprisal.

None of his employees had been killed in the warehouse attack on Chervonozoryanyi Prospekt, but financially it was a grievous blow. The hardware stockpiled there, much of it earmarked for the Right Front, had been worth millions of US dollars, maybe billions in Ukrainian *hryvnia*. A loss of that size pained him grievously. The thought of other losses still to come hurt even more.

At least he had a firm commitment from Samuil Skorokhod that the Right Front would assist in his defense. Skorokhod knew that without Britnev and his weapons, fighting for Ukraine would be an exercise in talking for the most part, while his soldiers craved the feel of automatic weapons in their hands and living targets in their sights.

The Russians might be coming anytime now, pouring over Ukraine's border any day, but first, before they faced that onslaught—and Britnev decided how to profit from it, one way or another—Skorokhod's commandos would be fighting on *his* side, protecting him, his operation and the steady flow of military contraband.

If the invasion came, of course, that trade would be disrupted in a heartbeat. Smuggling was a part of every war, but Britnev saw disaster for himself, a Russian born and raised, caught arming the resistance when the president's soldiers rampaged through Ukraine. At that point, he would have to turn his back on Skorokhod, return to singing the State Anthem of the Russian Federation, and strike any bargain that he could with the prospective victors.

Better still, he might just flee the region altogether, drop in on his several bulging bank accounts in Switzerland, and take his time deciding where on Earth to settle next, sharing his knowledge of deadly matériel with those in need of killing tools.

It was a wide world, after all, with no shortage of coups, rebellions, terrorism, civil wars, or ethnic cleansings.

Surviving this day was his challenge at the moment. Talking sense to Pavlo Voloshyn would do no good, when Britnev could not even speak to him in person. When the fighting started, Britnev hoped to get the first blows in and make them count, before the mobster could lash back and decimate his forces, possibly convincing the Right Front to cut and run.

One of his flunkies entered after knocking, without waiting for a summons. "What do you want?" Britnev demanded in a biting tone.

"You need to see the television, Boss," he said, tone deferential but excited, all at once.

"Which channel?"

"Any one with news on."

Britnev scooped up the remote, turned on his smart TV

and surfed through half a dozen channels until he found a news anchor running on about what seemed to be a terrorist attack in Obolon. A private home had been demolished by some kind of rockets, and two men were incinerated, nearly melted weapons found beside their bodies. They were thought to be the owner's caretakers, rather than the attackers. No name was available for the primary occupant as yet.

"That's *his* place, Boss!"

"His? Whose?"

"The hoodlum. Voloshyn."

"How do you know?"

"Our man with the police called in."

"Did we do this?"

"No, sir. I had some boys ready to do it, but you didn't give the order yet."

"Then who?"

His soldier shrugged and said, "Maybe Skorokhod?"

Britnev thought about it for a moment, shook his head. "No," he replied. "We were supposed to talk about a strategy before he moved against Voloshyn."

"Sorry, Boss. Then I don't know."

"Someone's done us a favor," Britnev said.

But inside his head, a small voice asked, Or did they only make it worse?

Podilskyi District, Kiev

MACK BOLAN'S TARGET in Podil that afternoon, as dusk bore down upon Kiev, lay two blocks northeast of the square on Spaska Street, directly opposite a park. It had been risky for Bogdan Britnev, stashing the victims of his human trafficking network in what some might have called plain sight, but the three-story house was old and well maintained, no eyesore that would draw complaints from neighbors who might call police.

The police, in any case, had been paid off.

Bolan and Sushko tried the more or less direct approach, both wearing knee-length raincoats in a passing drizzle to conceal their long guns as they walked from Bolan's rental to the front door of the venerable house. Sushko rang the doorbell and both men waited, hands on pistols through their coats' slit pockets, until a burly, balding doorman answered, growling, *"Chto ty khochesh'?"*

Instead of saying what he wanted, Bolan showed the guy, his Glock and Sushko's Makarov rising as one, a free hand shoving Baldy back inside. While Sushko closed the door, Bolan inquired, "How many other guards?"

"Ne Angliyskiy," the doorman answered, playing dumb.

Sushko asked him in Russian and the guy reluctantly said, *"Tri."*

"Three more," Sushko announced. "Or maybe two more, if he counts himself."

"Whatever," Bolan said. "Let's roust them out."

Shoving the front man in front of him, he barged into a parlor standing empty otherwise and put his Glock away, raising the AK-12 to fire a short and noisy burst into a nearby sofa. Instantly, they heard the sounds of footsteps hammering upstairs, then two men hit the spiral staircase to their left, descending rapidly.

Bolan dropped Baldy with a single 5.45 mm round to the head, as the man turned to make a play, then swung around to face the staircase, while the corporal raised his pump-action 12-gauge Bandayevsky. The shooters rushing to the doorman's rescue came into view mere seconds later, slowing just enough for caution's sake but not enough to save themselves.

Bolan stitched them from left to right, some half a dozen

rounds, while Sushko fired a buckshot blast that spread enough to cover both of them. The corpses tumbled down to ground-floor level, tangled up with each other at the bottom of the staircase in a spreading pool of blood.

"Careful of footprints," Sushko cautioned, as they stepped around the dead and started climbing to the second floor. Along that hall, a dozen closed doors greeted them, each one requiring clearance, taking time that they could ill afford. After the first two yielded seven frightened women cowering in corners, Bolan guessed the other rooms—and those above them, on the third floor—would reveal more of the same.

"We can't remove them," he told Sushko, "but your people can, if you've got someone you can trust."

"I know of one," the corporal replied, fishing his cell phone from a pocket. "I shall call him now." Before he rang off, they were back outside and moving toward the ZAZ Vida sedan. "I don't know what will happen to them, but at least we tried," he said.

"And we're not finished," Bolan answered. "Now it's getting real."

14

Vozdvyzhenka, Kiev

The millionaire's ghost town had not witnessed so many visitors in years. The new arrivals, all grim-looking males with bulges underneath their jackets, many toting heavy bags or obvious gun cases, parked their cars on side streets and fanned out as they had been instructed, jimmying their way inside unoccupied town houses where the furniture, if any still remained, was draped with sheets, awaiting the return of absent tenants.

Pavlo Voloshyn watched from a high window as his soldiers took their places, making ready to defend him at all costs. It was their oath-bound duty, and he had no fear that any man among them would renege and run away once battle had been joined.

As to that battle, Voloshyn had no doubt that it was coming. All the signs pointed in that direction, and he had been cautioned by a man he bribed within the Right Front that Samuil Skorokhod had answered Bogdan Britnev's call for help that very night. All told, Voloshyn reckoned eighty men or more were on their way to root him out and murder him, all based on what he now took to be a grave misunderstanding.

Stated plainly, he'd been framed, most likely by the rogue police corporal and his damned foreigner, still un-identified.

No matter. If they showed up on the killing streets this night, Voloshyn would learn the interloper's name.

And then, Voloshyn would begin repaying those who'd sent him to Kiev.

Three-quarters of an hour after the mobster's men were all in place, more cars entered the pricey ghost town, driv-ers of the latest fleet making no effort to conceal their ve-hicles. They parked along the curbs, some even in the street itself, as if to blockade the police and firefighters from re-sponding to alarms. They piled out, anywhere from four to six men in each car, and all of them were packing auto-matic weapons, shotguns, all the necessary killing tools.

They'd come for him, and the expressions on their faces told Voloshyn they were not open to negotiation.

Fair enough.

He waited, watching from his aerie, until Bogdan Britnev and his lapdog, Skorokhod, emerged from the backseat of a stretch limousine, a dozen shooters instantly surrounding them. Ready to start the party now, Voloshyn spoke into the Bluetooth headpiece he was wearing, linked to men in charge of every friendly unit stationed up and down the street.

"Begin!" he commanded.

On cue, second- and third-floor windows overlooking both sides of his street blazed with a storm of automatic weapons' fire. The first barrage dropped half a dozen Britnev soldiers and their Right Front comrades, scarring shiny vehicles with bullet holes and blowing out their tinted windows.

Down below, the shock troops scattered, seeking any cover they could find, returning fire in short bursts as they ran. More fell, some of them wounded, others lying deathly still, but there was still a goodly number of them on the move, apparently unharmed.

Voloshyn clutched his chosen weapon, a Bizon submachine gun packing fifty-three 9 mm Parabellum rounds in its unique helical magazine beneath its nine-inch barrel, capable of spewing slugs at seven hundred rounds per minute. If the invaders took him down, at least he would not die alone.

BOLAN AND SUSHKO watched the action from a rooftop they had scaled before Voloshyn's reinforcements had started to arrive, remaining out of sight until the large offensive force was in place and they could risk a look over the parapet.

"Voloshyn's doing well so far," Sushko observed.

"For now," Bolan replied, scanning the mobster's windows through his sniper scope. "Whatever happens on the street, he doesn't walk away from this."

Sushko grunted agreement and continued peering down at the battleground. "Britnev is hiding by his limousine," he said. "That's Skorokhod with him."

"Right Front?" Bolan asked. "Still in one piece?"

"Apparently."

"Let's see if I can do something about that," the Executioner said.

He swung the KNT-308 sniper rifle toward the longest car downrange, pockmarked by slugs, the shiny divots in its jet-black paint reminding Bolan of a robot with the measles. Britnev and Skorokhod huddled near the vehicle's left rear, partly shielded by its double back doors standing open wide in opposite directions.

It was not an easy shot, but those had never been Mack Bolan's specialty.

From where he sat, there were two ways to try the shot. First, he could put his bullets *through* the nearest of the limo's open doors, assuming they weren't armored against rifle fire, and try to hit the crouching men that way. Second, he could aim his bullets *underneath* the door. As glancing ricochets, there was a chance he could score against one or both of his selected targets. He might not kill them outright, but even a flesh wound from one of his 7.62 mm FMJ rounds could be crippling, potentially fatal if left untreated even briefly.

It was worth a try, in either case.

Bolan lined up his Steiner scope, relaxed into the trigger pull, and sent 122 grains of death hurtling toward impact with the pavement. It did not strike a spark but ricocheted as planned, a trifle off and striking neither of his human targets, flying on to penetrate the inside panel of the second open door.

Bolan simply made an adjustment after he had chambered another round, then squeezed off again. That time, despite the gunfire blazing from an arsenal of weapons up and down the street, he heard a cry of pain from someone crouched beside the limo, then the one who wasn't wounded bolted from his hidey-hole and ran for cover in a nearby recessed doorway, leaving his companion where he was.

Bolan recognized the runner: Bogdan Britnev. As to Samuil Skorokhod, and how badly he was hit, assessment would be stalled for the duration of the fight or until he got a closer look.

Meanwhile, the killing field was full of targets, offering a sniper's smorgasbord.

Bolan peered through his scope and focused on the feast.

THE LUCKY HIT on Skorokhod had spattered Bogdan Britnev with the wounded man's blood, prompting a gut reaction to escape before another bullet pierced their fragile hideaway. He'd made it to the curb and up into a sheltering doorway, but knew he could not hide there very long before some other shooter spotted him and tried again.

Britnev was carrying an OTs-12 assault rifle. Chambered for 9 mm rounds, with an eight-inch barrel and a folding stock, it could empty its 20-round box magazine in less than two seconds, assuming Britnev ever found a hostile target in his sights.

So far, all he'd been doing in the millionaire's ghost town was trying to survive.

Some of his men had not accomplished even that.

A glance across the street showed Britnev that his men had blown out several of Voloshyn's windows, other bullets scarring the facade of his stronghold. As to whether any of the occupants were dead or injured, he could not have said, but three or four were firing back from shattered windows, peppering the cars below with automatic fire. As he stood watching, someone tossed a hand grenade into the street, blasting the windows from a sedan.

He wished now that his men had brought heavier weapons, perhaps the Vampir RPG or the AT4-CS produced by Sweden's Saab Bofors Dynamics. Either one could blast their way into Voloshyn's castle, or reach out to set it blazing from the street, but Britnev had dictated small arms only and was now regretting his mistake.

Too late.

They'd find another way inside, and do it soon, before Pavlo or one of his remaining neighbors, though few and far between, called the police. Britnev had come prepared for war, but not against the national constabulary. It might come to that on some day in the future, if the government continued to ignore him, but for now the enemy before him was his one and only target.

Britnev had to rally his surviving soldiers while a decent number of them still remained and storm Voloshyn's fortress, either kill him in his lair or pitch him out into the street for execution underneath the street lamps. The result was all that mattered: the mobster lying dead at Britnev's feet.

Urgently, he issued orders into the headset he wore, waiting until the chief of each small unit called back to acknowledge. Now the clock was running down on Pavlo Voloshyn's life, and soon he would be nothing but a fading memory.

BOLAN HAD NO clear shot at Bogdan Britnev in the doorway where he'd hidden, and the man seemed happy to remain there for the moment, relatively safe from harm. Meanwhile, his men were shifting and regrouping, cautious with the bullets flying all around them from Voloshyn's home defense team, gathering as if to storm the mobster's fortress in a swarm.

"How many do you think he has inside there?" Sushko asked him.

"Hard to say. They're firing out of seven windows simultaneously, and they've got grenades. His spotters in the other building have the entrance covered, too."

"A hard assault, then."

"Hard enough," Bolan replied. "But I can soften it a little for them."

Following his glance, Sushko said, "Ah. The RPG."

As Bolan reached for it, the corporal said, "I keep expecting sirens."

"Won't be long," Bolan agreed. "I'd like to wrap it up before the uniforms arrive."

Bolan had braced the RPG-7 across his shoulder, loaded with a high-explosive HEAT round, when his sidekick said, "It just occurred to me. I probably have no job to return to after this."

"You can't be sure," Bolan told him, "but it could be worse."

"Hardly, if they arrest me on a murder charge or for the other things we've done."

"I have a contact at the American Embassy," Bolan replied. "A number and a name to drop, at least. When this is done I'll try to hook you up. A flight out of the country, with some cash to get you started someplace else."

Sushko was silent then, frowning, and Bolan put him out of mind, framing the doorway of Voloshyn's house in the launcher's UP-7V telescopic sight. He waited for the first Britnev assault team to begin their rush, advancing under fire, and only fired his rocket when they'd reached the mobster's doorstep.

With a mighty *whoosh* and flames boiling behind him in the launcher's backflash, Bolan's rocket whistled toward its mark, the secondary rocket motor lighting after ten meters, ramming the deadly arrow forward at a speed of 958 feet per second. It clipped one raider's head off his shoulders without detonating, then its warhead met the heavy door and mushroomed into smoky flames, hurling more bodies and their fragments out into the bloodied street.

"Door's open," Bolan told himself, half whispering, waiting for more of Britnev's soldiers to advance.

But some of them had tracked the rocket's course and had him spotted now, their weapons swiveling to spray the rooftop, driving Bolan and Sushko down behind its parapet. A swarm of hornets traveling at supersonic speed flew over them, warming the nighttime air.

"Time we were going," he told Sushko. "Want to join the party?"

With a jerky nod, Sushko replied, "I don't mind if I do."

Shevchenkivskyi District, Kiev

MAJOR SEMYON GOLOS was about to leave his office when the phone rang, his private line. Reluctantly, he answered it and had to hold the handset well back from his ear, wincing as the familiar caller screamed at him.

"Send everyone!" Pavlo Voloshyn cried. "They're killing us!"

"Who is?" Golos inquired, hoping the man was drunk and raving, but he soon heard gunfire rattling in the background, and the noise of an explosion somewhere close at hand.

"Them!" Pavlo bellowed. "Britnev and his henchmen! Dozens of them! Hurry, or you'll be too late!"

"Where are you?"

"At my home! Hurry!"

Angry and feeling nauseated in a heartbeat, Golos swallowed the rising bile and told Voloshyn, "I'll be there as soon as I can manage."

Cutting off the call before the mobster could launch into another round of cursing, Golos speed-dialed Special Services, the famed SWAT unit employed to counter terrorist attacks, seize drug smugglers and to suppress protests held by dissenters in the capital. He ordered every man assembled, dressed and armed for riot duty in the next five minutes. Those on leave but still within the city should be called in to augment the force and rush to Vozdvyzhenka as soon as they could manage it. From there, the sounds and smell of gunfire would direct them to the battleground.

And damn it, he would have to go himself, as well.

The Makarov PM pistol he carried was the major's only
weapon, but he planned to stop off at the arsenal before con-
tinuing to the garage below ground, picking up an AKMS
submachine gun for himself. He had not fired an automatic
weapon in at least eight years, but Golos knew he would
feel better with the SMG in hand while he directed his commandos into combat.

An illusion? Possibly. But at the moment, he would take
whatever he could get.

After he rallied the Special Services team, Major Golos
next should have alerted his superior, Colonel Avel Dontov,
but he did not phone the colonel. There was too much to
explain—why Voloshyn had called Golos directly from his
home, instead of using the police's public emergency number, how he knew Golos, and all that flowed from that—for
Golos to get sidetracked at the moment. Dontov might have
wished to come along and take command, which opened up
another can of writhing worms. He was corrupt, of course,
but lacked the personal relationship with Voloshyn that
marked Golos as Voloshyn's main contact on the force.

A blessing and a curse that had turned out to be. Golos
lived for the money, but tonight, he realized, it just might
get him killed.

Vozdvyzhenka, Kiev

BOLAN AND SUSHKO made it to street level, crawling to the
rooftop access door, then racing down the building's service stairs, mindful of traps along the way. Four of Britnev's
men had occupied the same building, seeking a straight
shot toward Voloshyn's home downrange, and they had
noted that the rocket that had bowled their comrades over
had come from the rooftop overhead. As Bolan reached the

second floor, one of them shouted at him from the hallway to his left and cut loose with some model of Kalashnikov.

Bolan dropped prone, hoping Sushko would do the same, framing the shooter in his AK-12's di-optic sight. He fired a 3-round burst and put the gunman down, just as three more charged out of rooms facing the street.

Behind him, Sushko fired a ringing shotgun blast that caught a second gunner in the chest and flipped him through a flailing backward somersault, blood misting in the air as he went down. While Sushko pumped his weapon's slide-action, Bolan was firing on the other two hardmen, more short bursts spinning them and dropping them together on the hallway carpeting.

The Executioner waited a moment, to find out if any other shooters would be popping out, then rose and joined Sushko as they continued down the stairs. On the ground floor, they turned back toward the rear of the house and exited that way, into a side street lined with empty vehicles left by the troops storming Voloshyn's place. Picking an alley to his left, Bolan began to work his cautious way back to the street that had become a killing ground.

Off in the distance, toward downtown, Bolan heard sirens *bing-bong-binging* in response to some emergency. It could be anything, but as the number and the volume of those sirens rose, closing on his location, Bolan didn't need a crystal ball to guess where they were headed.

"Shall we go?" Sushko asked.

"Not yet," Bolan answered.

"But the police…"

"I want to see how they respond."

"And if they target us?"

"With all that going on?" A nod from Bolan toward the raging battle made his point.

"But still…"

"Here's what you do," Bolan replied. "Stay here and watch. I need to find a way across the street."

"And if you don't come back?"

He tossed Sushko his spare key for the ZAZ Vida and said, "Use your best judgment. If it looks too tight, take off."

15

After the blast that killed a number of his men, Bogdan Britnev hung back and waited for the second wave to charge. When it advanced, he cautiously emerged from hiding in the doorway of a neighbor's long-abandoned home and made his way across the pavement, past his bullet-riddled limousine.

Samuil Skorokhod still lay where the rifle slug had found him, burning through his guts, but he'd stopped moving. The pond of crimson that he sat in looked like gallons spilled onto the street. His eyes, locked open, staring skyward, had already taken on a dusty look by light from the surrounding street lamps.

Britnev moved on, closing up the distance to his men as they entered Pavlo Voloshyn's house over the smoking ruins of his stout front door. They stepped in blood and offal as they cleared the threshold, none taking account of it as they all focused on the inner darkness, waiting to be ambushed by Voloshyn's home defenders. Britnev still had no idea how many were concealed in there, but he was going to find out.

He only hoped his soldiers and the Right Front paramilitaries found out first.

His OTs-12 rifle only weighed six pounds, with its loaded magazine included, but it seemed to drag on Britnev's arms as he approached Voloshyn's doorstep, dodging globs of flesh and organs in his hand-made Salvatore Ferragamo ornamented loafers. The combined stench of explosives and human remains gagged him, but he kept down his late lunch with a determined effort.

Once inside, some of his men fanned out to clear the ground-floor rooms, while others stormed the stairs. Shooting began almost at once, up on the first floor—called the second by Americans—where some of Voloshyn's men had grouped to make their stand against the enemy. Bullets ripped into walls and ceiling, raining plaster dust, and Britnev saw one of his men—or was he from the Right Front?—tumbling backward down the staircase like a dummy made of cloth or straw, shot through the chest and abdomen.

Against his better judgment, Britnev moved in closer to the stairs. He listened to the firefight raging overhead, considered whether he should turn and run, but let his courage win out in the end. With halting steps, he started up the stairs, clutching his rifle tight enough to make his knuckles ache.

When the grenade came out of nowhere, bouncing toward him, Britnev spent a wasted second gaping at it, then turned on his heel, prepared to leap over the banister and out of range before it blew. In fact, he was too late, had barely braced his free hand on the rail when the grenade exploded, lancing him with shrapnel from behind. The shock wave pushed him over, sent him tumbling through the smoky air and plummeting face forward toward the hardwood floor, where everything went black.

IN SEMIDARKNESS, SEVERAL of the street lamps shot out now, Mack Bolan slipped along the sidewalk for a block, then crossed over to reach Voloshyn's side, apparently unseen by either the attackers or defenders. Singsong sirens were within a quarter mile or less by now and gaining fast, as the police swooped down to shoot, arrest, or perhaps defend whomever they found living at the scene.

Once he had crossed the body-littered street, Bolan ducked down another alley and came around behind Voloshyn's mini-palace from the rear. Its tall back door was locked, but in the din of combat no one on the premises was likely to hear one more shot, so Bolan took the door's lock off and bulled his way inside.

The house was cool, its air conditioner still functioning, but gun smoke now pervaded its ground floor and had to be seeping toward the upper levels, winding up the stairs. Above him, on the second floor, he heard defenders battling the invaders, but had no idea which side was winning, though he guessed the housemen had to be outnumbered and outgunned.

Or were they?

Even as his thought took form, the echo of a hand grenade's explosion sounded from the general direction of Voloshyn's foyer, maybe on the staircase. Screams followed, and by the time he had a visual on that part of the house, more men were down, some of them writhing, others lying deathly still.

One of the latter faced Bolan, dead eyes staring from atop a broken neck. He recognized Bogdan Britnev and mentally crossed one of the top names off his target list.

And was Voloshyn still alive?

If so, he had to be somewhere upstairs, amid the firefight as it waxed and waned.

The wise course, Bolan thought, would be to exit as he'd entered, unseen by his enemies, and get the hell away from there with Sushko. On the other hand, if he decamped without proof that Voloshyn had gone down, his mission would be incomplete, and waiting for a bulletin from the police, perhaps delayed for days, was not the same.

He needed eyes on the mobster's corpse to satisfy himself. If that required a greater risk for Bolan, then so be it.

What else did he live for, after all?

PAVLO VOLOSHYN FIRED a short burst from his Bizon submachine gun toward the doorway of his private study, where he had retreated as the raiders burst into his home. Beyond the door, somebody screamed. No way of telling if the slugs had found a mortal spot or only caused a flesh wound. Either way, his adversaries knew he was prepared to fight, and they would have to think before approaching him directly.

But if they were carrying grenades…

Voloshyn shrugged that off. So far as he could tell, only his men had used grenades in the fight. Someone outside did have a rocket launcher, as he'd seen when it destroyed his front door, but that blast had killed his adversaries and he still had no idea who was behind it, since his men had not been armed with RPGs.

Another mystery, and at the moment, he was only worried about one: whether he would survive the next few minutes.

The police were was coming. He could hear the sirens growing close now. They would have to battle through his enemies outside, and if they wound up jailing some of his men for carrying illegal weapons, he would fight that battle later, in a court of law. None of it would matter if he died before the officers arrived to rescue him, and if his lackey Golos failed him…

What? Voloshyn could not dupe himself into believing he would be alive to wreak vengeance against the major unless he was rescued from the ruins of his home.

The millionaire's ghost town would be a *true* ghost town after this night, with all the lives snuffed out by violence. In some countries, he knew, that kind of thing would doom a neighborhood. Americans and Brits often dismantled the homes of their worst killers, leaving barren ground behind or building parks to pacify survivors, but Ukrainians—while still deeply religious in some quarters—did not cling to such outdated superstitions. Murder was not exorcised by bulldozing a house or an apartment complex, by renaming streets and trying to pretend nothing had happened, after all.

If ghosts existed, they would stay regardless.

Voloshyn, for his part, was moving out—if he survived.

Outside his den, he heard slithering sounds, as if someone was crawling toward the partly open door. He crouched behind his desk and waited, staring at the portal without blinking, and was ready with his Bizon when a cautious head appeared at ankle height, peering into the room.

This time he did not miss. The short burst from his SMG shattered the stranger's skull, spraying the hallway with his blood and brains. Behind the dead man, someone gasped, retreating from Voloshyn's line of fire.

Below him, in the street, the mobster heard squad cars screeching to a halt.

Salvation was approaching. All he had to do was wait.

MAJOR GOLOS STEPPED out of his cruiser, careful to let other officers precede him in the urban combat zone. No matter where he looked, bodies were scattered in the street, and he could see the marks of an explosion on Voloshyn's stoop, concrete blackened and blasted, more men torn apart, blood painted on the wall.

He had seen nothing like it before, and wished he could crawl back inside the squad car, simply tell his driver to reverse and get the hell away from there before the various combatants turned their guns on him. Instead, he watched and waited while his men engaged the battlers still outside Voloshyn's house, exchanging fire with them, disabling some and taking hits on their own side.

The men from Special Services were dressed and armed like soldiers: camouflage fatigues and flak vests, helmets with dark visors, combat boots and automatic weapons, pistols tied down low in quick-draw holsters on their thighs. They were highly trained and blooded in conflict with terrorists, dissenters, barricaded lunatics—but none of them had faced this kind of concentrated violence before, either, as far as Golos knew.

First time for all of us, he thought, and grimaced sourly.

As his commandos ringed Voloshyn's residence, advancing steadily despite their casualties, Golos began to creep along behind them, moving from one cruiser to the next and using them as cover for himself. His AKMS submachine gun was a burden, but it still made him feel slightly safer while advancing in a crouch, stooped low and waddling forward like an old man who had lost his walker.

Take your time, he told himself. *Commanders don't rush in and lead the charge.*

No fear of that in his case. He was terrified, each new step forward threatening to be his last. Golos feared that paralysis might grip him any second and humiliate him in the eyes of his subordinates, assuming that it did not kill him first. The only antidote to terror was advancing into danger, putting on a show—albeit fraudulent—of joining in the fight.

And when he wrote his report to his superiors, he'd be the hero of the day.

A medal might be waiting for him if he told the tale convincingly enough and no one contradicted him.

As if they'd dare.

So far, he had not fired a shot and meant to keep it that way for the moment. Once he was inside the house, secured by his advance troops, there would be time enough for posturing, asserting his command over the men who did the real fighting. But until then...

"Major!"

The voice called out from somewhere to his left. Turning, Golos picked out a lone man standing in an alley and beckoning to him. Why did the stranger look familiar?

Maksym Sushko! Golos had been staring at his service photograph a short time earlier, before the riot call.

Cautiously, clinging to his SMG, he turned and scurried toward the man whom Pavlo Voloshyn had commanded him to find.

MAKSYM SUSHKO WAS surprised at seeing Major Semyon Golos on the scene, when normally a captain would have been dispatched to lead the men of Special Services. His higher rank should have confined Golos to headquarters until the firefight was suppressed, when he would turn out in his uniform to meet the press. But since he *was* there, Sushko thought he'd seize the opportunity to warn Golos about Matt Cooper, tell the major just enough to keep his troops from killing Cooper, but without revealing any of the American's secrets.

Not that Sushko himself had much in way of secrets to reveal.

He *could* link Cooper to a list of lethal crimes, thereby condemning him to life in prison, but he still had no idea who had sent Cooper to Ukraine or whom he'd be reporting to if he escaped. Cooper had said he would not kill police, but in the heat of battle, could he keep that pledge?

"Major," he said, as Golos neared him. "I am glad to see you here."

"Corporal," Golos replied, "it has been difficult locating you."

Feigning a measure of surprise, Sushko answered, "I didn't know that you were trying, sir. If I may tell you—"

"Silence!" Golos snapped at him, raising his submachine gun and pointing it at Sushko's chest. "I ask the questions here. You answer."

"But—"

"One more word, except to answer me, and you're a dead man."

Sushko nodded his understanding, hanging in the shadows, his Bandayevsky dangling at his side, in his right hand.

"Now," Golos said, "where is the damned American who you've been working with?"

Surprised, Sushko tried bluffing. "An American?"

"Don't waste my time! I have my orders," Golos told him. "Pavlo Voloshyn won't be satisfied with double-talk."

As if he had removed a blindfold, Sushko saw it all. Golos was on the mobster's payroll, like so many other officers around Kiev and elsewhere in Ukraine. Whether he was the highest placed of those corrupted, Sushko could not say, and he had no time to think about it at the moment.

"Major—"

"If you lie, you die. Fair warning, eh?" Golos was smiling as he spoke the words.

Without a choice, Sushko dropped to his knees and raised his shotgun, squeezed its trigger and dispatched a buckshot charge that smashed the major's breastbone, blowing Golos backward from the alley's mouth and out into the street.

MACK BOLAN CLIMBED Voloshyn's service stairs, distinct and separate from those in front, and reached the second floor of Pavlo's house without incident. Once there, he found a handful of attackers clustered near a partly open door, their heads together, plotting strategy. Another man, nearly headless, lay before them, leaking blood and brains into the carpet.

Bolan had already seen the cops outside and knew these men in normal street clothes weren't with the regular police. He counted five men breathing and had no spare time to duel with them. Raising his AK-12, he sighted down the rifle's barrel and fired off a full magazine from thirty feet or less, before they noticed him.

The five went down, stone dead if not quite cut to ribbons by his 5.45 mm rounds. Bolan reloaded as the last of them collapsed onto the floor, blood mingling with the nearly headless corpse's offering. Jacking a round into the AK's chamber, Bolan moved up to the door that stood ajar and called through it in English.

"Pavlo, it's time to give it up."

"Who's that?" a ragged voice inquired.

"The bill collector. You've got tabs long overdue."

"You sound American."

"Got it in one," Bolan admitted.

"You must know that I was not responsible for the atrocity in Washington."

"Does it really matter? We're running out of time."

"*You* are," Voloshyn answered back. "The officers outside are friends of mine."

"I figured that." As Bolan spoke, he palmed an F1 frag grenade, released its pin and lobbed the bomb through the gaping doorway, toward the room's far wall.

If Voloshyn saw it coming, he did not react in time. The blast muffled his scream. There was a pattering like driving hail as shrapnel tore into the walls, then Bolan was inside the smoky den, moving to where the mobster was sprawled out on the floor beside his desk, facing the pock-marked ceiling. Once he'd kicked the Bizon out of reach, Bolan stood looking at the fallen mobster.

"Was it worth it?" he inquired.

"What do you know about me or Ukraine?" Voloshyn gasped, blood spilling from his mouth.

"I know you're guilty and the country doesn't need you. That's enough."

"You judge me, then?"

"I'm not your judge," Bolan corrected him, before the light died out behind Voloshyn's eyes. "I'm your judgment."

"Judgment?"

Bolan got it in under the deadline. "I'm your executioner."

Epilogue

Boryspil International Airport, Kiev

"This is goodbye, then," Maksym Sushko said.

"And high time, too," Bolan replied. "You should be glad."

"Much work must still be done."

"That's your job, not mine."

The dust was slowly settling from his mission. Sushko had explained killing the major to his bosses, bolstered by a stash of ledgers from Pavlo Voloshyn's safe that detailed payments made to Semyon Golos over time. Golos was not the only public servant on Voloshyn's payroll, but sorting out the others would take time and huddled backroom consultations. Bolan wondered whether any of the others would be brought to justice, but kept his reservations to himself.

His job was done, and he was going home.

"I am not a sergeant yet," Sushko said, "but I will be when the final Golos verdict is released. Perhaps I'll get a medal, also."

"No chance it will backfire on you?" Bolan asked him.

"None. The higher-ups require a scapegoat. Golos served hem perfectly, since he cannot speak for himself."

"Or point a finger up the food chain."

"Thus I am absolved." He cracked a weary smile.

"Good luck with cleaning up," Bolan replied.

A woman's disembodied voice called Bolan's flight for boarding, first speaking Ukrainian, then English, followed by a string of other languages.

"Is it bizarre to say that I will miss you?" Sushko asked.

"It passes. Get some sleep before you have to face any more questions."

"Yes, I will. You have a safe trip home, wherever that may be."

Bolan smiled wistfully as they shook hands, and said "I couldn't tell you if I tried."

* * * * *

UPCOMING TITLES FROM

DON PENDLETON'S
THE EXECUTIONER

OMEGA CULT
978-0-373-64450-6
March 2017
After a devastating sarin-gas attack in Los Angeles,
Mack Bolan follows North Korean terrorists back to their
home country—where he must rout the billionaire leader of
a splinter sect to stave off nuclear warfare.

FATAL PRESCRIPTION
978-0-373-64451-3
June 2017
A wealthy industrialist is about to release a lethal virus and
use the antidote as a ticket to the Oval Office. It's up to
the Executioner to take down the madman's mysterious
assassin and stop the pending epidemic...

DEATH LIST
978-0-373-64452-0
September 2017
Mack Bolan poses as a high-profile assassin to penetrate
an organized-crime ring, but the game is up when he and his
look-alike show up at the same meet. Bolan may have met
his match, but there's only one Executioner.

ROGUE ELEMENTS
978-0-373-64453-7
December 2017
A ship carrying nuclear materials disappears after leaving
North Korea, and the private security firm hired to protect
it comes under scrutiny. Mack Bolan goes undercover to
infiltrate the corrupt security company and find the
missing uranium.

CNMGE0916R

SPECIAL EXCERPT FROM

THE **DON PENDLETON'S**
EXECUTIONER.

Check out this sneak preview of
COMBAT MACHINES
*by **Don Pendleton**!*

Bolan realized he couldn't hear the man's footsteps anymore.

He was too far into the Metro tunnel for the light from the platform to do him any good. Slipping his hand into his pocket, Bolan grabbed his smartphone and pulled it out just as he heard the scrape of a shoe.

He turned toward the noise just in time to get his jaw almost torn off by a powerful kick that made stars explode in his vision and sent him to his knees. Even so, he managed to lash out with a fist, but connected with nothing except air.

"You can't win, you know." The voice, light and mocking, echoed in the tunnel, seeming to come from all around him. "Who are you—an American? Are you the best they could send?"

"Yeah, I am. Who are you?" Bolan asked as he slowly rose to his feet.

"I'm something you cannot even begin to comprehend." Shoes scraped over gravel, and then another heavy blow struck Bolan, this one on the back of his lower leg. "I'm the next generation of warrior, far superior to you and your obsolete kind."

The far-off rumble of a train echoed down the tunnel.

and a glimmer of light pierced the darkness from around the bend.

"In fact, since you're so obsolete—" The man delivered a hammerblow to Bolan's kidney, knocking him to his knees again. Bolan fired at where he thought the guy should have been, but again his strike found only air. "I think it fitting that you die right here."

The assassin hadn't moved very far away, and Bolan seized the slim opportunity. Raising his smartphone, he triggered its camera, which also set off the auto flash.

As he'd hoped, the bright light in the man's face blinded him, and he staggered backward.

The light from the train now illuminated the tunnel, and Bolan saw the man's silhouette a few yards away. He charged forward, intending to tackle him and bring him down, but just as he was about to get his hands on him, the man spun aside as he slammed his fist into the back of Bolan's head, driving him to the ground, stunned.

Bolan tried to push himself up, tried to crawl over to the narrow space next to the tracks, but his arms and legs refused to obey his commands. The train's headlight was blinding now, overwhelming his vision, the thunder of its approach drowning out everything.

His last thought before the blackness took him was that this was not how he'd expected to die…

Don't miss
COMBAT MACHINES by Don Pendleton,
available December 2016 wherever
Gold Eagle® books and ebooks are sold.

www.Harlequin.com

GEXEXP0916